MARIE FERRARELLA

Cavanaugh on Duty

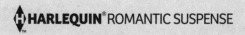

HARLEQUIN® ROMANTIC SUSPENSE

Recycling programs
for this product may
not exist in your area.

ISBN-13: 978-0-373-27821-3

CAVANAUGH ON DUTY

Printed in U.S.A.

Books by Marie Ferrarella

MARIE FERRARELLA

This *USA TODAY* bestselling and RITA® Award-winning author
has written more than two hundred books for Harlequin Books, some
under the name Marie Nicole. Her romances are beloved by fans
worldwide. Visit her website, www.marieferrarella.com.

To Ian Conrad,

Welcome to the world, Little Man

Prologue

Something was wrong.

He could feel it in his bones, smell it in the air. The minute Esteban stepped out of the run-down tenement apartment building he'd called home these past three years, he'd sensed it.

Something was off.

He had nothing concrete to base it on, except for a gut instinct. The same gut instinct that had helped him survive out here on the cusp of hell, slowly making his way up the cartel food chain, earning trust by seemingly not giving a damn.

It had been a juggling act all the way. The people within the drug cartel had an honor code without displaying a shred of real honor. Moreover, they expected a man to keep his word while they broke theirs with bone-chilling regularity.

Black was white, and white vacillated between non-existent and a color he couldn't begin to describe.

But he had managed to navigate these streets, being one of them while standing apart, and all the while sleeping with one eye open.

Although it had come at a great personal cost, he'd bided his time, waiting for the chance to even a score that would never truly be even.

But this *thing* he was feeling was different. His nerves twisted and tensed; a chill swept along his spine. Every fiber in his body was on high alert, listening intently even though he didn't know for what.

And then he knew what he was listening for.

Because he heard it: the high-pitched whine of a bullet as it hurtled from its source.

A bullet with his name on it.

Abruptly, he swung to the right.

The bullet couldn't.

It missed him.

The same gut instinct told him to keep on running if he wanted to live. Confronted with an actual choice between life and death, he surprised himself by deciding to live a little longer.

So he kept on running.

His job wasn't finished. He still had people to bring to justice. After that, it didn't matter what happened to him. He was already dead on the inside anyway.

Chapter 1

Brian Cavanaugh leaned back in his chair as he studied the young man in his office. *Intense* was the first word that sprang to mind, prefaced by *very*.

His own words were measured when he spoke, as his goal was to put the other man, freshly plucked out of undercover work, at ease.

"The first thing I want you to know is that this is not a demotion—"

It had been an exhausting thirty-six hours, beginning with a nerve-racking leap from the very jaws of hell. Esteban's surroundings right now—clean, orderly, devoid of vermin—seemed almost surreal. He'd all but forgotten places like this existed.

But he'd chosen that netherworld over this because he had a purpose, a mission. The mission wasn't accomplished yet. He needed to find a way back. Somehow.

"With all due respect, sir, when someone leads with that, it usually means that it *is* a demotion," the man who had gone by the name Juan Dominguez for the past three years pointed out.

The corners of Brian's mouth curved in apparent amusement. "You mean like when someone prefaces a statement with the phrase, 'With all due respect,' he or she usually doesn't harbor that respect?"

Unable to contain his restlessness, the detective who'd been summoned to Brian's office continued to pace. His broad shoulders stiffened slightly. "I wouldn't know about that, sir. In this case, there is a great deal of respect. It's just that—"

"It's just that you feel as if you've been given a time-out, sent to stand in the corner, while everyone you know is still out on the playground, doing what they please," Brian guessed, completing what he anticipated were the younger, somewhat disheveled-looking man's thoughts on the matter.

"Something like that," the detective murmured. He returned the Chief of D's look, searching for an opening, a way to reverse what he knew in his gut the older man was planning on doing.

"You know you *can* sit down in my office," Brian reminded him patiently. He'd already extended the invitation to the man whose real name, according to the requisitioned file on his desk, was Esteban Fernandez.

Esteban stopped pacing. His tone was polite, with just a hint of defiance, as he asked, "Is that an order, sir?"

Brian had not reached his rank by choosing his battles recklessly. This was not a battle, just a reassessment of a situation. Fernandez could be either a valuable asset—or a loose cannon.

"No, just a point of fact," he replied calmly.

"Then if it's all the same to you, sir," Esteban said, "I'd rather stand."

"Actually, it's not," Brian told him, his eyes holding Esteban's. "But if you prefer to imitate a moving target, that's your call."

Esteban watched the Chief for a long moment. According to what he'd heard, Brian Cavanaugh was considered fair to a fault by the men and women who answered to him and whose undying allegiance he'd earned one by one.

Esteban wavered for a moment, wanting to stick to his guns, an army of one. Then, suppressing the sigh that rose to his throat, he lowered his lean, muscular frame into one of the two chairs that faced the Chief of D's desk.

Brian smiled. There wasn't so much as a hint of triumph in his voice as he said, "Thank you, Detective."

Esteban barely nodded, bracing himself as he waited for the inevitable shoe to fall.

The wait was almost nonexistent.

The Chief of Detectives' next words were the ones Esteban had been dreading for thirty-six hours, ever since Manny Diaz had opened fire on him. Part of him still didn't know how he'd survived.

But there was *no* part of him that didn't want to go back.

"You're being pulled off the undercover assignment, Detective."

Esteban winced.

He'd been preparing for this meeting, for these damning words, ever since he'd been made less than two days ago. That was when he'd been identified as an undercover cop rather than a drug dealer with a growing clientele.

Made or not, he wasn't about to accept this decision quietly. "Sir, I could still—"

The Chief cut him off before Esteban could waste any more breath, because that was all that it would be. Just a waste of breath. His mind was made up. Not because he was an egotist who enjoyed wielding power, but because he was not about to allow any of his people to risk certain death. Life was far too precious for that.

"No, you couldn't," Brian said firmly. His voice was not without compassion as he continued, "You were made, Detective. There is now a price on your head. A price that doesn't carry the option of 'dead or alive,' just 'dead.'" He leaned forward over his desk, creating an aura of privacy between himself and the young detective. "Jorge Lopez doesn't like being made a fool of…and discovering an undercover law enforcement officer operating as a dealer right under his nose makes him out to be a *huge* fool. He wants your head on a pike in order to save face."

Brian lightened his tone. He didn't want to strike fear into his detective's heart, just arouse his dormant common sense.

"Call me selfish, but I'd prefer having your head just where it is. You're being pulled out to save your life, Detective. As good as you are—and according to everyone who counts, you are *very* good—you won't be any further use to us with a target on your back. So, unless you have a death wish, you will accept reassignment as graciously as you can.

"This is a good thing, Detective Fernandez," Brian continued. "A lot of men who came before you and went into undercover work never got the chance to get out. At least, not alive," he amended.

Esteban struggled to keep his reaction to the Chief of D's words from showing on his face. He didn't want to be gracious. He just wanted to continue doing what he'd been doing: getting rid of scum one drug dealer at a time. It was the only thing that gave purpose to his life.

"Yes, sir," Esteban bit off, staring past the Chief of D's head.

Brian heard the animosity in the other man's

voice—could almost feel it. But he wasn't here to make friends at the expense of a man's life. Even a single life was one too many.

His eyes held Esteban's. "You don't sound as if you believe me."

It wasn't that he didn't believe the Chief, it was just that he had no desire to play it safe, to get out of the game where he risked his life daily, betting that very same life against some pretty steep odds that he would see another sunrise.

"No, sir, I do believe you." He cast about for the right way to say this. Maybe he actually had a shot at changing the Chief of D's mind on this after all. "It's just that—"

"You're afraid of being bored to death," Brian said. When Esteban looked at him in surprise, Brian allowed himself a moment to laugh. "I didn't guess at that, Detective. I've been in your place. Granted, it feels like a hundred years ago now, but I worked undercover when I was about your age. In my case, it was to take down a sex-trafficking ring selling innocent, underage girls to the highest bidder. Trust me," he continued, "I'm familiar with the adrenaline rush that comes from a job well done, a deadly exchange foiled, detection narrowly avoided. Can't bottle that or find a pill to evoke the same kind of feeling.

"That comes from seeing firsthand that you've saved a life, maybe several lives, and prevented someone else from being kidnapped in the future. Doesn't matter that that person will never know that, because of your efforts, they've been spared. All that counts is that they *have* been spared."

Esteban looked at his superior with newfound respect. He hadn't been aware that the Chief had ever actually walked the walk. "You were involved in something like that, sir?"

"I was and I know what a comedown it feels like to be handed a job that you feel an overage, half-witted Boy Scout could handle with one hand tied behind his back. But in all honesty, that feeling is unwarranted, not to mention inaccurate."

Listening intently, Esteban waited for Cavanaugh to continue.

"Aurora," Brian pointed out with pride, "seems like a sleepy little burg only *because* of the unending vigilance of the men and women in the police department, the officers who patrol and the detectives who piece together the puzzles."

Brian took a breath, allowing his words a moment to sink in.

"So, to reiterate, this is *not* a demotion, but a lateral promotion. There's been a recent opening in the Homicide Division."

Brian paused again, trying to ascertain the best approach to winning this man over. There was no doubt in his mind that Fernandez was an asset. But an asset who needed to have his focus redirected—and that didn't promise to be easy.

"We lost a good man two weeks ago," Brian stated bluntly.

"In the line of duty?" Esteban asked, sensing that the Chief of D's was waiting for him to respond in some way.

"Out of the line of fire," Brian quipped. "Detective First Class Ernest Lau made it to retirement age and the second he did, his wife insisted that he stop pressing his luck and leave the force."

"What's he planning to do?" Esteban asked, not because he was the least bit curious, but because he sensed that this, also, was expected of him. He had gotten to where he was—and lived to talk about it— because he had the instincts to intuit in most cases what was expected of him in either deeds or words.

"Not get shot at anymore, for one."

The answer hadn't come from the Chief of D's, but from the woman crossing the threshold directly behind him. Esteban turned in his chair to glance at this newcomer walking into the Chief's office.

It wasn't Cavanaugh's administrative assistant. He knew because he'd passed the woman when he'd initially entered the Chief's office. He'd noted that she looked like an attractive, contained woman in her late forties. This woman walking in looked as if she'd just popped out of a Cracker Jack box a few seconds ago, and the experience had clearly invigorated her to go on popping.

How did she figure into this? Esteban wondered,

even as he had the sinking feeling that maybe he really didn't want to know the answer to that question.

She also looked the slightest bit familiar.

Had their paths crossed?

And if so, when?

How?

For the past three-plus years, he'd dealt strictly with people who either were the dregs of society or had *dealt* with the dregs of society on a regular basis.

If anything, this perky, peppy, blue-eyed blonde would fall into the second category. And yet...

And yet he wasn't all that certain he knew her in that capacity, either.

Maybe he didn't know her, Esteban decided a second later.

For now, he would let it be. If he did know her, well, then he'd find out soon enough one way or another. It was just that simple—and possibly, just that complicated. What it *wasn't* was worth his time wondering about it.

"You sent for me, sir?" she asked genially, directing her question as well as her attention to the man behind the desk.

She was also doing her very best *not* to stare at the other man in the room.

Even so, she couldn't shake the feeling of recognition that had instantly come over her.

That was Steve. It *had* to be, she thought.

If it wasn't, then it was his doppelgänger. No one

else she knew had hair like that, so black that it almost looked as if it had steel-blue highlights woven through it.

And those intense blue eyes—they'd come from his mother, she recalled hearing him say once. Those same eyes were responsible for melting an entire squad of cheerleaders in high school, not to mention almost every other teenage girl within a five-mile radius of the hunky, popular quarterback.

God knew she hadn't been immune to him either, but she'd had no desire to beat off a throng of adoring, salivating females just to get a little one-on-one time with the devastatingly handsome football player.

Funny thing about that. She'd always thought he would make a name for himself in the professional arena, but he seemed to have completely disappeared shortly after he'd graduated high school. They'd been exactly a year apart, even though she had shared a couple of classes with him.

Was this where he'd ultimately wound up? Working in law enforcement and looking like someone badly in need of a haircut and a shave, not to mention new clothes?

Maybe it *wasn't* Steve, she thought, reconsidering. As she recalled, the heartthrob of the gridiron had a grin that had a way of imprinting itself on the souls of every female, young *and* old, whom he ever came in contact with.

This man in her newly discovered uncle's office had

a somber, almost sullen expression. It was the kind of expression that told the casual observer that he didn't know *how* to smile.

She directed her wayward attention back to her uncle. The latter smiled warmly at her as he gestured toward the empty chair.

"Please, take a seat," he urged. When she did, he undertook the introductions. "Detective Esteban Fernandez, I'd like you to meet Detective Kari Cavelli-Cavanaugh." He paused for a moment to allow the names to sink in on both sides, then he added the all-important words, "Your new partner."

Esteban visibly balked, his impassive expression cracking just long enough for his complete displeasure to show through.

"Sir," he protested, "I haven't worked with a partner for three years."

"Then it's high time that you did," Brian told him matter-of-factly. "You've more than earned the right to have someone else watching your back."

Brian could see that the news was not being received well, but then he'd known it would take time. Rome wasn't the only thing that hadn't been built in a day. Neither was trust. But it all started with taking the first step. And this was Fernandez's first one, even if he abhorred it.

"Your lone-wolf days are over, Fernandez, so you might as well get used to it."

The expression on his handsome, tanned face was

far from accepting. "Sir, could I have some time to think about this?" he asked in a clipped voice.

Brian shrugged. "You can take the time it'll take you to go home and clean up."

For form's sake, the Chief pretended to glance at his watch. He was well aware what time it was. It was one in the afternoon. Fernandez had come to him straight from the safe house he'd been whisked to when he'd had to flee from the run-down apartment he'd been renting from his contact to the cartel.

"Tell you what," Brian amended. "You can take until tomorrow morning to decide." He knew he'd be doing the detective a disservice if he didn't offer this option.

"But be aware of the fact that there's nowhere else I can put you right now, so your choice, I'm afraid, is limited to yes or no," he said as Esteban rose to his feet. Getting up as well, Brian leaned over his desk and shook the other man's hand. "I'd hate to lose you, Detective," he added with conviction.

Esteban had lived the past three years exclusively in a world where lip service was commonplace and actions spoke far louder than anything that could be said.

Still, despite his wariness of the spoken word, Esteban had the feeling that the Chief was being sincere. It didn't change what he felt was going to be the ultimate outcome of this meeting, but it was still nice to be appreciated, even if just for a fleeting moment.

"Think long and hard, Detective," Brian counseled somberly.

"I plan to, sir," Esteban answered.

Deliberately avoiding any eye contact with either the Chief of D's or the pretty blonde in the room, Esteban strode out of the office.

Kari watched in silence as the detective walked away. She was still debating whether or not this was the same person who had created such a stir in high school eight short years ago.

His gait was different, she decided. But the set of his shoulders… That definitely reminded her of the Steve she knew. She had a feeling that if she came right out and asked whether he'd attended Aurora High School at the same time that she had, he would just find a way to stonewall her.

No, this was going to require a little detective work on her part.

Kari made a mental note to dig out her yearbook when she got home and look through it.

Right now she was still on the job. Sort of. Turning around, she faced the man whom she had recently established a personal connection with and looked into his eyes.

Never one to beat around the bush, she said, "He's planning on turning you down, you know."

It was nice to know that gut instinct and intuition were alive and well in the next generation, Brian thought with satisfaction.

"I know," he replied. "I also know he doesn't have anything else in his life." Brian had always made it a point to know everything that was pertinent about his people and about those who were going to become his people. Detective Esteban Fernandez was no exception.

Then this *couldn't* be the Steve she'd gone to high school with, Kari decided. *That* Steve had had a mother, a stepfather and a younger half brother he'd doted on. Julio had come to cheer him on in *all* the football games.

She'd only been a detective for a short while, but she had learned very quickly how to read her superiors without making it seem as if she was trying to second-guess them.

"Would you like me to see if I can change his mind for you?" she asked.

For his part, Brian did *not* answer yes or no. What he did was tell her simply, "I'd like you to be Kari."

It was enough.

She smiled, inclined her head and said, "Yes, sir," before turning on her heel and leaving his office.

She had people to see and information to gather.

Chapter 2

Kari focused on her assignment the moment she walked out of the Chief's office. As far as she was concerned, it was unspoken but understood that she could avail herself of all the resources she needed in order to bring Detective Esteban Fernandez back into the fold.

Being a Cavanaugh certainly had its perks, Kari couldn't help thinking with a smile. Because there were so many Cavanaughs in the actual police department, as well as various offshoots—such as the D.A.'s office—she had access to places and entities she hadn't even known existed before she discovered her connection to the large family.

Technically, *she* hadn't actually "discovered" the connection—she, along with the rest of her siblings, had been told about it by her father, who also happened to be the head of the CSI day unit. He'd called a family meeting shortly after he'd been informed by none other than Andrew Cavanaugh, the former Aurora chief of police, that he was actually a Cavanaugh.

According to Andrew, her father, Sean, had been the victim of a distraught nurse's error. Reeling from the news that her fiancé had been killed serving overseas, she'd completed her rounds in a total emotional fog. It eventually came to light that during this time he and another male infant, born on the same day and having the same first name and the same first three letters of the last name, had accidentally been switched.

The end result was that her father had gone home with Mr. and Mrs. Cavelli, while the Cavellis' real son had gone home with Shamus Cavanaugh and his wife.

Her father had grown up completely unaware of the mix-up, but secretly haunted by the strange feeling that something was off in his life. Not to mention that he didn't resemble any of his four siblings.

Meanwhile, Kari and her family eventually found out that the real Sean Cavelli hadn't grown up at all. He'd died in infancy, long before his first birthday, throwing the woman who ultimately turned out to be her grandmother into an all-consuming depression. That mental condition was compounded by the fact that even before the SIDS death had occurred, Martha Cavanaugh had maintained that the infant was not hers. That he was *not* the child she'd given birth to and held in her arms in the delivery room.

No one had paid any attention to her, thinking that she was just suffering from postpartum depression as well as the guilt and emotional trauma that went with losing an infant to what was then termed "crib death." It wasn't until more than four decades later, long after Martha had died, that she was proven right. The infant who had died *wasn't* her son.

The discovery that the infants had been switched at birth threw both families into emotional tailspins. The various members on both sides dealt with the news in their own ways. The ones who were most affected, of course, were the Cavellis. Not only did the revelation create turmoil, but it also caused each of her six siblings as well as her father to suffer through their own personal identity crises.

But, unlike some of her siblings, finding out that she was actually a Cavanaugh did *not* throw Kari for a loop or cause her to stay up nights, questioning who she really was in the grand scheme of things. She accepted the change in status cheerfully, seeing it as an expansion of her base family.

In her heart, she was still a Cavelli—because to her, family had never just been about DNA or bloodlines, it was about a connection, a state of mind. Consequently, she only saw the upside in being related to the

Cavanaughs, a large, prominent family most of whose members were dedicated to the principle of protecting and serving the citizens of the city in which they lived.

As far as Kari was concerned, one could never have too much family. A big, extended brood meant there was always someone to talk to, someone to side with you. Someone to have your back.

Happily, a large family also provided a wealth of connections to be tapped into. And that was exactly what she intended to take advantage of now in order to track down Fernandez's permanent home address.

Or to at least find out where the man got his mail delivered when he wasn't deeply immersed in the drug cartel. She reasoned that before he'd gone underground for the good of the department, he had to have hung up his clothes *somewhere*...and she intended to find out where that "somewhere" was located. Because with any luck, that was where he was now, weighing his options and contemplating his choices.

She intended to convince him that there was only one conceivable option with his name on it.

Brenda Cavanaugh, married to the Chief of Detectives' son, Dax, was the police department's reigning computer tech nonpareil. Though there were several other techs within the small department, if information was possibly obtainable, she was the one who could find it. To Kari's way of thinking, even though Esteban Fernandez's life had been off the grid for more than three years now, he'd initially lived somewhere

under his own name. She was confident that Brenda
would know how to backtrack and find it.

She was right.

Within twenty minutes of her inquiry, the Chief
of Detectives' daughter-in-law had discovered where
Kari's decidedly reluctant parter-to-be had lived before supposedly vanishing.

"Why didn't you just go to HR?" Brenda asked
curiously as she handed Kari the address she'd just
printed out.

"Too much red tape," she answered. Besides, as far
as she knew, there were no family members in HR.
Kari believed in using leverage whenever she could.

Glancing at the address, she folded the paper in
half. Fernandez lived closer to the precinct than she'd
thought. In fact, his place was on her way home.

Perfect.

"Besides, I don't think I'm supposed to actually
get my hands on this information without some kind
of authorization," she confessed.

"And yet, you did," Brenda said, pointing out the
obvious. "Why come to me with this request?"

"Other than the fact that you're a freakin' genius
when it comes to finding things via the internet?" Kari
asked without a hint of a smile on her lips.

Brenda's grin was wide enough for both of them.
"Other than that fact, yes."

Kari nodded at the paper in her hand. "The Chief

of D's wants me to change this detective's mind about handing in his shield."

"And you're planning on ambushing him at home, where he thinks he's safe."

Kari bobbed her head. "Like I said, you're a genius." However, despite the accolades, she could tell that the other woman wasn't exactly gung ho about the situation.

True to form, Brenda indicated the paper she'd just handed to Kari. "As long as you know that you didn't get that from me…" she cautioned, clearly wanting to distance herself from any possible fallout. With the ease of an unobtrusive pickpocket, using only her thumb and two of her fingers, Kari folded the paper into quarters until it disappeared entirely inside her palm. Then she unselfconsciously slid her hands into her pockets and smoothly deposited the paper with the address she'd requested.

"Get what?" she asked in complete innocence.

Brenda merely laughed and then waved her away. "Go. I've got work to do," she told her unexpected visitor.

"I'm already gone," Kari reassured her.

The next moment, opening the first door she came to, Kari made good on her promise.

Esteban frowned, mulling over his present situation and its apparent lack of options.

He had no idea what he was going to do with himself from here on in. Getting justice for his family had consumed all his time and energy for so long—ever since Julio's overdose more than three years ago—he had no clue where his mission ended and he began. At this point, they were one and the same, and without this single-minded purpose, it was as if someone had sucked all the air out of his lungs…depriving him of the very will to breathe.

Now what? he silently demanded of the darkness around him.

The police department didn't want him to work undercover anymore—and he knew why. They didn't want him getting killed on their watch.

But he himself had no such concerns, no such worries shackling him. Death didn't scare him. Inactivity was what scared him.

He *had* to be doing this, making a difference where it counted, doing everything in his power to bring down the cartel and its brethren, so that no one else's brother or child would be discovered dead on the floor of their room after OD'ing on drugs.

And, by extension, he was doing this so no one else's father would be grief-stricken enough to go out, half-crazed, and hunt down the dealer responsible for the overdose, killing him in cold blood and suffering the consequences of that action: prison for twenty years.

Maybe, Esteban thought as he poured himself another two fingers' worth of whisky from the bottle he'd unearthed earlier, he could just become a crusader, fight these bastards on his own.

He didn't need the police department's blessings to do this, he mused, urging himself on. Fact of the matter was, he could accomplish this mission without them. He had a little money saved up and didn't really require very much to live on.

The idea appealed to him.

He'd become an avenging angel.

"No," he corrected himself out loud, "an avenging devil." Because men like the one his stepfather had shot dead only understood a show of force. In this case, the show of force would be put on by a man whose soul was as black as theirs.

Maybe, in its own way, blacker.

"That's it," Esteban decided with a firm nod of his head, "I'll be an avenging devil."

He laughed, relishing the sound of that.

The next second, the laughter died in his throat as he froze. Immediately, his hand covered the hilt of the service revolver—his backup piece—that he'd tucked into his waistband before he and the bottle of whiskey had sat down together.

He'd heard something.

Someone was knocking on his door—the bell had long since given up the ghost and he'd had no reason to fix it. Visitors weren't welcome.

Instantly alert, he stealthily made his way over to the front door in the dark. He saw no point in switching on any of the lights and giving whoever was on the other side of the door enough illumination to target him. The fact that his potential killer would announce himself by knocking on the door seemed completely plausible to him. Acting in a normal fashion was meant to throw him off, to quiet any of his suspicions that might arise.

At the door now, Esteban held his breath, anticipating whatever might happen next. He slowly drew his weapon out, holding it at the ready so that if his unexpected "caller" decided to break in, he'd be right here, waiting for him—

"Fernandez?"

His eyes narrowed as he stared at the door, as if that could somehow help him see whoever was on the other side.

The voice clearly belonged to a woman, but that could still be some sort of a trick, a way to get him to relax his guard—

"Fernandez? Are you inside there? It's me. Cavelli-Cavanaugh, or just Cavelli…if that makes you more comfortable. Are you in there?" she asked again.

Kari had already circled the perimeter of the forty-year-old home once, and she had seen the car that she'd identified as the detective's. It was parked over on the next block rather than in front of the house—by force of habit, no doubt.

But whether or not it was habit didn't matter. What *did* matter was that the hood was still warm, but not hot. That meant that Esteban had driven it over sometime after he'd left the precinct.

That in turn meant that he was here.

"I come bearing gifts, Fernandez," she informed him in a tone that was infinitely sweeter than the one she typically used day-to-day. "C'mon, open the door," she coaxed, then added, "unless you want me to pick the lock, of course—because I do know how to do that."

Of course she did, Esteban thought darkly. He'd intended to wait her out, but that course of action was quickly aborted when he saw the doorknob jiggling.

Muttering a curse under his breath, Esteban quickly released the locks and yanked open the door. His weapon was not only out, but ready, in case the woman the Chief of D's was trying to push on him was here under duress.

But when he opened the door, he saw no one else but her. The shimmering moonlight, out in full force, had turned her skin almost a golden hue.

She belonged in someone's dream, not on his doorstep, he thought in annoyance.

And it looked as though she was doing this of her own free will. It figured, he groused to himself. They weren't even going to let him quit in peace.

Seeing a drawn weapon, Kari's immediate reaction would normally have been to pull out her own service revolver, but she had no desire to exchange fire with the potently sexy man she'd come to coerce.

With effort, she managed to silently talk herself down and keep her own weapon holstered.

There was absolutely no light coming from inside the house. Had the streetlamp behind her been out and with a new moon in the sky, she wouldn't have been able to see her unwilling partner at all.

"Are you raising bats or orchids in there?" she quipped, crossing the threshold. "Or did you just not pay your electric bill?"

From the surly look on his face, she could tell he wasn't in the mood to exchange banter. He clearly wanted to be left alone.

"What are you doing here?" Esteban bit off, making no effort to hide his hostility. After all, the woman was invading his space, a space she wasn't even supposed to know about.

Can't trust anyone these days, the former undercover detective fumed.

"Not being welcomed for one," she answered glibly.

His eyes narrowed. "Then go home. No one's stopping you."

"And turn my back on such a charming invitation?" she deadpanned. "No way."

He had no idea what she was talking about. Somewhere, he was convinced, a village was searching for their idiot. Just his luck, she'd turned up here.

"*What* charming invitation?" he muttered.

Kari remained blissfully unfazed by the daggers his eyes were shooting at her.

"The one you silently extended to me back at the precinct. You know, indicating that you wanted me to share a drink with you," she answered. As if to reinforce her point, she held up the bottle of expensive whiskey she'd thought to bring with her. "I even brought the bottle in case you didn't have any—or started without me and ran out."

That, she felt, was a pretty safe bet. Leaning slightly forward, she gave him her best, most innocent smile. "But I see that you did remember to pick up a bottle on your way home."

He was *not* about to get sucked into this mindless babble. He just wanted to be left alone, to get drunk out of his mind, pass out and not think for a while. This highly annoying Pollyanna was interfering with his plans.

"Look," he ground out, "I don't have time for crazy women—"

"Good, neither do I," she concurred. Feeling her way around the room, she found a light switch and turned it on. Illumination instantly flooded the room.

"Turn it off!" he ordered.

But she didn't. Instead, she informed him blithely, "Just looking for another glass." She opened one cabinet, then another. Both were empty. This man lived worse than a hermit. "You do have another one, right?" she asked, looking over her shoulder at him. "Otherwise, one of us is going to have to drink out of the bottle."

Esteban stared at the woman in his house, feeling like someone who had just been slammed by a runaway train that had come barreling out of nowhere. She still hadn't answered his question.

"How the hell did you find out where I live?"

"I'm a very resourceful person," Kari told him with a wide grin. "You'll find that out when we start working together."

"We're *not* going to be working together," Esteban snapped. This was like some bad dream that refused to fade. Did he have to bodily carry her out of his house to get rid of her?

"Of course we are," Kari countered brightly. "Fighting the inevitable is just a waste of time and energy. You like being a cop, I like being a cop and right now, the Chief of Detectives wants us to be cops together." She looked at him as if he should have known that he couldn't win this battle. "He always gets what he wants."

The look he gave her was darker than any look she'd ever seen on a perp's face. "Not this time he won't," he growled.

Chapter 3

The woman who had brazenly invaded his much-needed solitude smiled at him as if his strongly voiced protest was destined to fall by the wayside.

Outraged by her impertinence, Esteban could feel his already-fanned flames of anger swiftly growing.

He was well aware that he was physically strong enough to simply toss this golden-haired irritant with the sexy mouth out of his house, but, even with more than half a bottle of bourbon in him, Esteban didn't want to resort to the behavior of the very lowlifes he was attempting to get off the streets.

However, if he ever was inclined to give a woman the bum's rush, it definitely would have been this vexing thorn in his side.

"Who sent you?" he demanded, his eyes darkening into a frown. "The Chief of Detectives?"

She wasn't about to hide behind her uncle, or allow Esteban to think she was nothing more than a puppet, obediently doing what she was told. So, rather than say that Brian Cavanaugh *had* indirectly asked her to bring him into the fold, what she told Esteban instead was, "I came to find out why you don't want to work with me."

Which was in actuality *part* of the reason why she was here.

Esteban looked down contemptuously at the bottle of aged bourbon she'd brought with her. "So you thought, what? That you'd liquor me up and I'd tell you everything?"

She looked at the bottle she'd placed on the counter out of the way while she searched for another glass. "No, this is to fortify me so I can put up with you," she told him bluntly. "But as I already offered, you're certainly welcome to share it with me if you'd like." She lifted her bright blue eyes to his. "I might have a lot of faults, but stinginess is not one of them."

Esteban's expression remained inscrutable. She caught herself holding her breath, waiting to see if she'd managed to burrow her way into his inner sanctum at least a little bit.

"Is that supposed to impress me?" he wanted to know. "Your bravado?"

If she blinked and backed off, Kari knew that she'd

lose any chance of making the tiniest bit of headway with him. And as for gaining any ground, well that was just an unfulfilled fantasy at this point.

So, with nothing to lose, she decided to duke it out instead. "I don't know, is it?"

Esteban uttered a sound that was a cross between an intolerant, short laugh and a contemptuously dismissive one. And then his eyes darkened again as they swept over her.

The same strange note of familiarity whispered through him with no more clarification than the last time. Except that this time the thought that she was damn attractive and too sexy for his own good insisted on taking root.

"You don't want me working with you," he warned.

There was absolutely no hesitation whatsoever on her part. "Sure I do."

"No," he repeated firmly, his voice almost ominous in timbre. "Trust me, you don't."

She had never accepted *anything* at face value or just because she was told to. She'd always needed proof, ever since she was very young.

It was no different now.

"Okay, I'll bite. *Why* wouldn't I want to work with you?"

As she spoke, Kari poured herself two fingers of bourbon, taking it neat, then offered the bottle to him.

Esteban poured twice as much for himself into his glass, then tossed it back quickly, making it disappear between his lips all at once. His eyes, watering ever so slightly, were the only indication that the alcohol intake had even affected his body at all.

"Because you come on like some prep-school educated Barbie doll, and I'm not going to pretend to be Ken," he informed her.

Before he had a chance to take another swig from her bottle, Kari laid claim to it, her lips lightly touching the rim as she tilted it back.

"Good," she pronounced once she'd swallowed. "Ken has fake hair," she reminded him matter-of-factly, as if she was talking about an actual living, breathing being instead of an iconic doll. "I never really liked Barbie's boyfriend." She held the bottle out to him again. "Don't worry. I won't get in your way."

"Especially if you're not there," Esteban agreed flatly.

Kari shook her head. What the hell had the Chief gotten her into? "You are a hard devil to get close to," she commented.

Now she was finally getting it, he thought. It was about damn time. "Not hard," Esteban corrected. "Impossible—and I like it that way."

She laid it out for him, although she was certain that he'd already figured this out on his own. What did he hope to gain by playing this little charade out? Did he think this was going to "put her in her place"? Establish their hierarchy in relation to one another?

"Well, it's either partner with me or hit the road,

and I think you've invested too much time into the job to just walk away. At the very least, you'd have to start all over again somewhere else."

He paused his ongoing communion with the bottle she'd brought. His own—the one he'd opened tonight—was now empty and he wasn't finished drinking. He was still standing. "I really don't care *what* you think, Ms. Cavanaugh."

"It's Detective Cavelli-Cavanaugh," she corrected him, deliberately slurring just a bit for his benefit.

Her apparent inebriation was, for the most part, staged. The drinks she'd been taking from the bottle, now that they had both forgone the niceties of actual glasses, were deliberately exaggerated in appearance. In reality, it all amounted to very little alcohol going down. Kari had no intention of getting drunk—and it wasn't because she was worried about the regretful events that might consequently follow once she reached that state. Rather, it was because she just knew that if she couldn't appear to hold her liquor, he would have even less respect for her than he did now.

And the point of this entire confrontation was to get Esteban to have a decent amount of respect for her, not less.

"Hell of a mouthful," he muttered, referring to her hyphenated last name.

Kari smiled at him, the kind of smile that hinted at secrets being held back. "Yes," she told him, "Actually, I am."

"Think a lot of yourself, Cavelli-Cavanaugh, don't you?" he asked, mocking the extralong name.

"Not a lot," she assured him, then added, "just my due. And you can pick one of my last names to use. Just be consistent."

He stared at her in stunned silence for a moment. And this time, when the laughter came, it was heartier and not quite so full of animosity. He'd already had more than his fair number of shots before this beautiful, ornery woman had descended on him bearing a liquid peace offering. He'd lost count by now just how much he'd consumed.

The upshot of it all was that, while he wasn't feeling any more receptive to her now than before, the hostility that he did have—not so much against her as against the fact that he was being barred from continuing the work that had been his sole reason for living these past few years—was morphing into something else.

Something equally as strong and, from his somewhat detached point of view, equally as useless.

Something that, he was fairly certain, had he not been on his way to total intoxication, he would have been unaware of.

Namely that he felt attracted to this annoyance with the sexy legs. Not mildly or conveniently attracted, but teeth-jarringly, mindlessly, *intensely* attracted.

For the past three years, he had conducted his one-man crusade to bring down the men behind his half brother's drug overdose—and his stepfather's subsequent prison sentence—to the exclusion of everything else. This exclusion included not tending to any of his other needs beyond occasionally eating and sleeping… and he only paid nominal attention to those two things so he'd have enough stamina to continue working. Everything else—searching for creature comforts, entertaining desires of the flesh or even, moderately, of the soul—had been so completely neglected that they were just shut out as if they didn't exist.

But they did.

And now, for some unknown reason that utterly confounded him, he felt a flare of desire in this woman's presence. A flare of desire that didn't just evaporate the way he'd fully expected it to, but went on to spread like a wildfire through his veins.

To spread and feed on itself, and before he knew it, this raging desire threatened to take possession of him entirely.

Esteban was staring at her as if he hadn't seen her before, she thought, as she tried to understand what was happening. Was that the alcohol at work, or was he just trying to intimidate her into leaving?

It's not that simple, partner. You can't get rid of me that easily.

"You shouldn't be here," he barked at her.

"You already said that. Have we run out of conversation so soon, throwing us into some kind of verbal reruns?" she asked wryly.

He had no idea what the hell she was talking about. He just wanted her out of here. *Now.*

"No, you *really* shouldn't be here," he told her. But even as he said it, he drew closer, like an imminent danger from which there was no escape.

He was so close now that when he uttered his warning, she could literally *feel* his words on her skin, words that were wrapped up in his warm breath.

The lethal combination made her heart quicken. Had she been completely sober, and not slightly tipsy as she was right now, a red flag would have shot up for her instantly.

As it was, the flag did go up, but it went up in what felt like slow motion—and once it was up, it seemed to wave in a rather happy, lackadaisical manner.

Truth be told, she was far more fixated on the sensations erupting between them in the wake of this moment of unexpected physical closeness. "And why shouldn't I be here?" she asked him, raising her chin a bit to defiantly punctuate her question.

Or maybe, she silently reconsidered, she wasn't being defiant. Perhaps she was merely flirting with him.

Or at least the bourbon was, she amended.

Esteban realized in frustration that the words needed to explain why it was imperative that she go *now* seemed to have escaped him. But then, he'd always been a man of action rather than words anyway.

Even back when his world had been incredibly shel-

tered in comparison to his life now, he was more prone
to doing than talking.

So rather than search for words that wouldn't come,
and an explanation that refused to present itself, Esteban *showed* her why she needed to leave.

More roughly than he'd intended, he took hold of
her cheek with one hand, keeping her in place as he
brought down his mouth on hers.

This kiss was meant to scare her away.

Instead, what he actually managed to accomplish
was to scare *himself* away—but not before he took the
so-called "warning" he was issuing to its full conclusion, devouring her the way a starving man devoured
his first meal in countless days. Except that for Esteban, it had been countless months, not days. Countless
months that had stumbled their way into years without his complete recollection of that empty journey.

Pleasures of the flesh hadn't been important to him
at the time.

Now, though, something seemed to be stirring
within him....

This uninvited woman he found himself saddled
with tasted of all the good things that he had con-
sciously left behind the day he'd found his brother
Julio dead on the bedroom floor. She tasted of for-
bidden fruit, the fruit a man like him had knowingly
sworn off in exchange for the life he'd dedicated himself to leading.

A life that, if conducted correctly, would allow him

to get rid of at least a few scum of the earth before he himself was terminated. That the last part was inevitable, he was well aware of. But he didn't care as long as he took as many of them with him when it happened—if not before.

Oh wow, oh wow, oh wow.

This time she had gotten more than she had bargained for. Maybe even more than she could possibly handle, Kari realized.

It felt as if her very soul was being sucked into a heated vortex.

The smart thing, she knew, was to push this man away and run for her life. But that presupposed that her knees and legs were still working—which they weren't. Both had turned to mush of varying consistencies.

Besides, she didn't really feel all that compelled to do the smart thing anyway. Not when it involved pulling away from what was the surprisingly delicious feast of his mouth.

Yes, the man, even in his scruffy state, was sexy and attractive to a fault, but who knew this lay beneath it all?

Her reluctant partner's kiss left her feeling a hell of a lot more intoxicated than the amber liquid she had brought with her. The latter did not hold a candle to what he could accomplish with that mouth of his.

So, just for a moment longer—or so she tried to convince herself—she allowed herself to linger.

And linger.

Kari closed her arms around the man's neck, leaning her body into his and patiently waiting for the kick of that mule that had somehow managed to sneak into all this to subside.

It didn't.

If anything, it increased.

And, to her utter surprise, she had no complaints.

He hadn't survived these last three years by allowing his emotions, or the sensations that were at times generated by those emotions, to decide his path for him. *He* was the one who forged the path, the one who kept himself safe in the most *un*safe situations.

He didn't do it letting down his guard by so much as a sliver.

That took strength. Strength he knew he had to tap into now.

So it was with superhuman effort that Esteban put his hands on her shoulders and pushed Cavanaugh's niece away from him. "Get out of here," he growled, secretly afraid of where the next step might take him. He had no room in his life for more regrets.

Kari stood her ground. "No."

Her defiance temporarily threw him for a loop. He stared at her, as if not comprehending her negative response to his order.

What the hell was wrong with her?

Did she think this was easy for him? Being noble wasn't exactly his calling.

"Get the hell out of here," he repeated, his voice more malevolent now than it had been before. "I don't think either one of us is ready for the consequences if you stay."

She didn't want to go. She wanted to stay, to see what happened. To see exactly where this would go and what she would feel when it got there.

Kari wavered inside, more than ready to deal with *any* consequences if this wondrous condition could be persuaded to continue.

But she had a feeling that what she felt here wasn't important. Esteban was the important one in this scheme of things. He was the one she'd been sent to convince to remain in the department any way she could. She wasn't fool enough to believe that if what was happening between them at this moment was allowed to go on to its logical conclusion—if they wound up making love—then he would remain.

She knew damn well that the exact opposite would occur.

If they made love tonight—and the promise of that was something she ached for with her entire being— then Esteban would disappear by morning, most likely never to be heard from again. Kari could sense that in every bone in her body.

So she banked down all the unleashed emotions

that were now madly unfurling within her. She was struggling to hold them in check, struggling to keep herself from throwing her arms around Esteban once again and pulling him back to that hotbed of sensual heat their coming together had generated.

"All right," she said thickly, doing her best not to suck in air as she spoke, but to take it in slowly and calmly. "I'll go," she agreed, then flippantly added, "It looks like we're out of alcohol anyway, so I guess the party's over for tonight."

He barely glanced in the direction of the bottles. "Looks like," he muttered in agreement. Anything to get her to leave—before he gave in to temptation and refused to let her walk out.

Taking a deep breath, Kari did what she could to center herself.

"You don't have to bother showing me to the door," she told him sweetly. "I can see myself out."

Esteban merely nodded. "Wasn't planning on it," he retorted.

At least he was honest to a fault, she thought, though she would have preferred to hear a token protest from him.

But then, since he was so honest, she would always know where she stood with him.

If he became her partner.

She nodded in response to his last words, turning to leave. She stopped for one more second, looking at him over her shoulder.

"And you'll be there tomorrow morning? At the precinct?" she added when he'd made no response to her question.

When he still remained silent, she took a step back toward him, her hand on her hip as she waited for him to say something.

He didn't want her walking back in. What had caused him to kiss her was still very much with him, and this time around, he was fairly certain that kissing would be the least of it. The stakes were definitely set to go higher, and he had no idea just where—and *if*—it would stop.

"Yeah, I'll be there," he told her curtly, ready to say, to promise, *anything* just to get her to leave. To get her out of harm's way before he did something that both of them would live to regret. "Now, go!"

She ignored his last words, focusing only on the first part. "Good," she pronounced. Her hand on the doorknob, she uttered one last parting shot. "Just remember, I know where you live."

Then, to forestall any further exchange—or, more important, any further temptation—she closed the door and left.

Chapter 4

Every time he walked into the state prison on visitor's day, Esteban could feel a slight tightening in his chest. All his senses would go on high alert and he became even more aware of the details of everything that was going on around him, including each person within his line of vision.

It was more than just his survival instinct going into high gear, the way it did when he was working undercover.

Because every time he walked through those prison gates, the thought *There but for the grace of God went he* would echo through his brain and continue to do so until he was back in his car, driving away from the prison.

Esteban was well aware of the fact that it wouldn't have taken much for his life to have gone off on a different path. At the very least, if he'd been home instead of away at school, he might have been murdered, as his mother was. But most likely, he would have been in prison now the way his stepfather was, because he would have been the one who had killed the dealer who'd sold drugs to his stepbrother.

The drugs that had cut short his young life.

Except that, unlike his stepfather, Esteban wouldn't have stopped there and turned himself in. He would have wiped out everyone he came in contact with, everyone who'd had even the slightest connection to the drug ring and the distribution of that poison. He didn't flatter himself and think he was invincible. Either the drug dealers or the police would have eventually taken him down, but he would have wiped out a lot of worthless scum before he went.

He went on automatic pilot as he was being processed for entrance to the visitors' common room, enduring the metal detector, the pat-down, and emptying his pockets for the guard to rifle through. He didn't like having his things pawed over, especially by a guard whose condescending look made him itch to take a swing and wipe that superior expression off his face.

Esteban realized that his hands were still clenched

into fists at his sides, even though he'd entered the communal room and was now waiting for the guards to bring in the prisoners who had visitors. Exhaling slowly, he unclenched his fists.

The door to the communal room opened. After a beat, the prisoners, marching in single file, were allowed in. His stepfather was the fourth in line. Raising his hand, he waved to the man.

The moment Miguel saw him, his somber, lined face broke into a wreath of smiles, making him appear years younger. Sitting at a table, Esteban waited for him to cross to him.

Was it his imagination, or was the man getting frailer looking?

Esteban willed himself to relax, to drain the tension from his body. Seeing him upset or tense would only concern the man who had stepped up all those years ago to become, for all intents and purposes, his father. The only father he would ever know.

"Hello, Father." Esteban greeted the slighter man with a warm smile.

"Hello, my son. You came." Pleasure erased the weariness and etched lines from his face. "I didn't think you could."

His stepfather vaguely knew about his line of work, knew that he had to be careful about coming here because it could blow his cover. But even so, he found a way to come as often as he could.

And each time he did, each time he saw the pleasure in the older man's yes, Esteban knew it was worth everything he risked just to connect with Miguel one more time.

"How could you have any doubt?" Esteban asked. "You know if there's any way to be here, I would find it."

Miguel looked around, noting who was near them. Life here had taught him to be very cautious. It was always better to take too many precautions than not enough.

"Yes," he said in a low voice that carried only to his stepson, "but I also know that there isn't always a way. And if you cannot come, I understand. I worry," he admitted, because he knew without being told that Esteban lived his life in the line of fire daily, "but I understand."

"Stop worrying about me—start looking after yourself," Esteban advised. "You look a little pale, Dad." Esteban slid to the edge of the seat, getting in as close as he could, since there was a table between them and he knew better than to do *anything* that might attract even an iota of extra attention. "Something I should know about?" he asked.

One of the guards had ridden him these last few days, but he didn't want Esteban getting involved. This was his problem to deal with, his time to serve. The lawyer Esteban had managed to get for him had gotten his sentence reduced, wielding the term "temporary insanity due to grief" like a sword, but it could cut away only so many brambles. He was serving a twenty-year sentence and would be out in ten if he could continue maintaining his good behavior. That meant, among other things, not rising to the countless provocations that were seeded in his path.

Or sharing too much with the man he'd raised as his own. Miguel shook his head. "Just getting over a cold. Nothing to worry about. Really," he underscored when the furrow along Esteban's brow deepened. "How are you doing?" he asked, deliberately changing the topic. The tactic was not wasted on the younger man. "Watching your back at all times?" It wasn't a question but a reminder.

He'd forgotten. He hadn't been able to see Miguel since his narrow escape.

"They pulled me out, Dad," Esteban told him matter-of-factly, placing no more significance on this newest action than he would have had he been a shoe salesman and gone from selling men's shoes to women's. It was understood that there could be no details forthcoming, but he wanted the man to know he could stop worrying about his exposure. At least that aspect of the danger was over. "I'm working with a partner now."

"A partner?" Miguel echoed, well pleased. "Tell me, what's he like?"

The corners of Esteban's mouth curved ever so slightly as he refrained from giving his stepfather the first answer that came to him. *A real pain.* "Well, first off, he's a she."

"A she?" A twinkle entered the tired brown eyes. "That has to be a nice change for you, no?" Miguel speculated.

No was the immediate response, but again, he let it slide. He probably wasn't being all that fair to the woman. In any case, he'd give this forced alliance a little time to take before he made his final judgment.

"We'll see," Esteban told his stepfather. He glanced at his watch. "I don't think we've got that much time left." He smiled at Miguel. "I just wanted to stop by to see how you were getting along in this hellhole. See if you needed anything."

"Just for you to be safe. That is all I want. Now that you are doing something 'different,' I will be able to sleep again at night," Miguel told him. "And as far as hellholes go, some of the others here tell me it's not so bad."

"Still, all it takes is one guard, one inmate who has your number..." He didn't want to dredge up any details to frighten Miguel, just make him aware that there could be problems even down the line. "And if anyone gives you a hard time, I don't care who it is, you'll tell me, right?"

Miguel looked at him with an innocent smile. "Who else would I tell?"

The answer made Esteban even more skeptical than he already was. Miguel would keep the fact that someone was on his case a secret, just to protect him. That was the kind of father he was. But he didn't want him having to endure anything. Just being locked up was difficult enough on the man.

"Dad—" There was a warning note in his voice.

The buzzer sounded, calling an end to the visit. "I have to get back to my cell," Miguel said, using the sound as an excuse not to answer his son. "Come again when you can. Looking forward to your visits is what keeps me going," the older man said, rising from the table. *"Vaya con Dios, mi hijo,"* he said just before he fell into formation again. Within moments, the orange line was marched out of the common room.

Y tu tambien, Padre, Esteban thought, watching Miguel leave. "And you, too, Dad," he murmured out loud.

For what felt like the umpteenth time, Kari glanced up from her desk to the one butted against hers and sighed.

The chair facing hers was still empty.

The desktop was glaringly clear, save for the run-of-the-mill computer monitor and the single white coffee container perched in the middle of the scarred tabletop.

The coffee was her combination welcome-to-the-job/peace offering.

The dark-roasted blend that she'd picked up at a local coffee shop and placed on what was to be Esteban's desk was probably cold by now. Standing unattended for over an hour, even though there was a lid on it, did that to any drink, even one that had started out scalding hot.

She had gotten it on the way to work because she thought Esteban might appreciate something a little better than the sickly brown liquid that came out of the precinct's vending machines and was laughingly passed off as coffee.

She made the choice going on instinct rather than any information she had gleaned. When she'd gone to Brenda for Esteban's address, she'd also asked for any background information on him that might be available. There was none.

Technically speaking, that actually hadn't been exactly the case. There was some information, but whatever had been originally written down on the page had subsequently been redacted. Every line of type had been run through with a black permanent marker that promised not to disappear or fade over time.

So she had gone with her gut. Men like the one she'd met with last night—the man she still thought *could* be the Steve Fernandez she'd gone to high school with—didn't care for any frills. That included fancy rhetoric and coffee that bore a longer, fancier name than some people she knew.

The coffee was black…just like the mood that was slowly coming over her.

When she'd departed his house last night, she'd

been fairly confident that she'd gotten Fernandez to come around, to connect with her on the most basic level. Having her body tingle for more than an hour after she'd left him had been a small price to pay.

But now she was beginning to think that maybe she'd been wrong about his coming around, and it bothered her more than she cared to admit. To her way of thinking, she'd dropped the ball.

She didn't like letting the Chief of D's down, not because he was her uncle—or because she felt she had something to prove so she'd move up the food chain within the department. She didn't like letting the Chief down, because he'd asked her to do something and she wanted him to know that she always delivered on her commitments.

This was the first thing he'd actually asked her to do, and she'd failed.

Granted, it was still early. The workday had barely started, but all that translated to was more time in which to feel like a colossal failure.

She'd arrived at the precinct almost an hour earlier than she was supposed to, anticipating Fernandez's arrival. For her, the minutes had already stretched themselves out as thin as thread, each inching by as she waited for Fernandez to walk into the office.

It promised to be a very long day from where she was sitting.

"New guy not here yet?"

Startled, it took Kari a second to collect herself

before she turned around to look at the man who had somehow managed to come up behind her without making a single sound.

The question had come from Lieutenant Tim Morrow, a rumpled, unimpressive-looking former vice detective with yellowish-white hair and a waist that was slowly becoming wider than the breadth of his shoulders. Morrow had worked his way diligently through the ranks.

At the moment, the lieutenant was looking at the empty chair opposite her own, but his expectant manner, as well as his question, was directed toward her.

She wondered if Morrow knew about her visit to the Chief of Detectives yesterday.

Of course he did, she upbraided herself the next moment. If Fernandez was supposedly going to be working for the department, Morrow would have been notified of everything pertaining to the former undercover detective.

Had she and Fernandez already *had* some sort of working relationship, she would have been quick to attempt to cover for him, giving Morrow some sort of plausible excuse as to why the other man wasn't anywhere within eyeshot. Loyalty was something that was inbred in her, thanks to her father.

But since she didn't know if Fernandez was even going to bother showing up at all, she felt no allegiance…no urgent need to cover for him.

"'Fraid not," she replied to the Lieutenant's question.

Although it was obvious that Fernandez wasn't there, it was clearly *not* the answer that Morrow wanted to hear. He frowned, turning toward her. "You two are up," he told her.

For the first time, she saw the paper the lieutenant was holding in his hand.

Since this was the department that dealt with homicides and questionable deaths, she assumed that a call had come in and that the lieutenant had written down the address and a few scattered details on the notepaper he was holding.

"I can go alone," Kari volunteered, already on her feet. "Won't be the first time," she added needlessly to the man who had been in charge of training her when she'd first walked in through the precinct doors.

The story went that when Morrow had first arrived from the academy, Andrew Cavanaugh, who had gone on to become the chief of police before eventually retiring early to focus on raising his kids and searching for his missing wife, had trained the then-rookie cop.

What goes around comes around, she thought.

Pulling on her jacket, Kari put out her hand for the address.

"I'd rather there were two of you," Morrow said even as he surrendered the sheet of paper. "But since you're initially just checking out a bad smell—"

"A bad smell?" Kari repeated, puzzled. Since when had the police department started concerning itself with garbage detail?

"Yeah. Manager at a storage facility said one of the renters came to him complaining that there was a, quote, 'really bad smell' coming from the unit located right next to his." His far from narrow shoulders rose and fell in a resigned shrug. "Could just be some food someone was stupid enough to stash away. Or an animal that had the bad luck to crawl into the unit when the door was open and became trapped inside, eventually expiring. Or—"

She noted that the lieutenant only awarded the dignity of death to people. Everything else "expired," like a container of milk going sour, or a warranty on a product.

"Or a body someone had stashed in the unit while they tried to figure out how to make it disappear without calling attention to themselves," she concluded for her boss.

Morrow nodded, his unruly, longer-than-regulation hair falling into his squinty, deep-set brown eyes. "Exactly."

"Mind if I hope it's fruit until I find out otherwise?" she asked.

The weather was turning unseasonably warmer. That meant that a body hidden in a storage unit was bound to decompose more quickly than usual. This was *not* an assignment she was looking forward to.

"It's a free country," the lieutenant replied magnanimously.

Kari glanced at the address before tucking it into

her pocket. The storage facility wasn't located far from the precinct, she noted.

Securing her weapon, she was just about to leave the office when she saw the look of surprise that fleetingly passed over the lieutenant's craggy face. Since the man was facing the outer door that led to the hallway, she turned around to see what had caught his attention.

No wonder he looked surprised, she caught herself thinking. Esteban Fernandez created quite an imposing impression at first sight.

And even second and third, she mused.

To be honest, at first glance he didn't even look like the man she'd spoken with last night. That man had been scruffy and raw. This one fell under the category of "tall, dark and handsome." But there was still a dangerous edge to him despite his clean-shaven face. An enticing, dangerous edge.

But then, last night he was still embracing his other persona, the undercover cop he'd been—a role he'd played for the past three years, if the rumors were correct. And, at this point, that was all she really had to go on. Rumors. Law enforcement detectives involved in the undercover world did not exactly have readily accessible data that the regular force could easily refer to. Whatever they did was not supposed to ever see the light of day or be acknowledged—good or bad.

She made a mental note to take another crack at the Cavanaugh pipeline. So many of the Cavanaughs were involved with the various departments at the precinct, it only stood to reason that *someone* had to know *something* viable, something she could use when dealing with the man she assumed was going to be her new partner.

However long that association lasted, she did *not* want to be in the dark or at a disadvantage when it came to dealing with this man. At the very least, she wanted to know exactly *who* she was trusting to have her back.

"Fernandez?" Morrow inquired, obviously as stunned by his transformation as she briefly had been.

Esteban glanced over toward the lieutenant just as he reached his desk—since the desk was so blatantly empty, except for the computer and the coffee container, he'd made a logical deduction that it was going to be his.

For as long as he decided to remain here, he silently added as a footnote to placate himself.

"Yeah?" he asked the lieutenant.

Morrow looked far from pleased with this latest addition to his department. "It's customary to report to your commanding officer when you first join a department," he said, his gravelly voice rife with displeasure.

"Sorry, sir, I just now walked in," Esteban pointed out needlessly. Right before he'd visited Miguel in prison, he'd made his decision to continue his association with the police department until he could figure out how to get back into undercover work. He'd gotten caught in morning rush-hour traffic on the drive back from the penitentiary, which accounted for his less than timely appearance.

His eyes met Kari's and he gave her what amounted to the smallest, most imperceptible of nods, acknowledging her presence.

It was a start, she thought.

Kari heard Morrow grumble almost inaudibly under his breath. All she caught was something that made a vague reference to his retirement still being too far off. Then the man said more distinctly, "No time to make small talk right now. You and the hyphen here are up. She's got the address. I'll talk to *you* later," he emphasized, looking accusingly at the newest member of his team before he went back into his glass-enclosed office.

"The hyphen?" Esteban repeated, looking at Kari. He'd told himself that for the most part, after last night, he was just going to ignore her, but for once his curiosity got the better of him.

"Cavelli-Cavanaugh," she reminded him. "It's hyphenated."

He shook his head in disbelief. The last three years his very survival had depended on traveling under the radar, not attracting any attention to himself. He saw her name as being the exact opposite.

"You're really using both?" he asked her.

To Kari, it was the only logical way to go and it made perfect sense.

"Since I thought I was born the one, but was really born the other and there's family attached to both names, I figured…why not?" she asked.

Esteban shrugged indifferently in response to her rhetorical question. "Makes no difference to me," he told her. "I don't care what you call yourself as long as you answer if I call you."

This, she thought, was going to be one hell of an interesting partnership—for as long as it lasted, and she still had her doubts it would live out the week, given his attitude.

"By the way, coffee's yours," she told him just as he was about to walk back toward the doorway.

Esteban stopped and regarded the container with less than enthusiastic interest. "I didn't—"

"No," she cut in, anticipating what he was about to say, "but I did." Then, just in case he wasn't following her—or possibly wasn't even listening to her—she clarified, "I bought coffee for you. Sort of a welcome-to-the-department offering," she explained before Fernandez could ask her why she had bothered to buy him coffee at all.

Esteban picked the container up and fell in place beside her.

"You were that sure I was going to come in?" he wanted to know. If that was the case, that put her one up on him, he thought, since *he* hadn't known he was coming in until a couple of hours ago.

"You said you would," she reminded him, leading the way down the hall to the elevator.

His laugh was dry and completely devoid of humor. "And you believed me?"

She would be the first to admit that she was entirely too trusting in her dealings with people. As a detective, that worked against her. As a human being, though, she felt it didn't.

"You haven't given me a reason not to yet," she replied.

"The day's still young," he countered. He took the lid off the container and took a sip of the black brew. "It's cold," he told her. It wasn't a complaint so much as an observation about the state of the liquid. Hot or cold, as long as the coffee was black, he wasn't fussy. It all went down the same way.

"It wasn't when I got it," she told him pointedly.

It was a little after eight now. She must have come in before then. "Which was—?" He deliberately left it open for her to jump in.

She saw no reason not to oblige him. "At seven this morning."

"You not only expected me to show up, you actually expected me to be early?" he asked incredulously.

Reaching the elevator door, they stopped and she pressed the down arrow on the tiled wall.

"Seemed like something you might possibly do, at least on your first day," she answered.

Her eyes swept over him and she was again struck

by the fact that this clean-cut man hardly looked like the man who she'd barged in on last night.

The man who had also briefly set fire to her world, she caught herself thinking with no small longing right now.

She'd promised herself not to dwell on that, Kari reminded herself sternly. However, the memory refused to fade. Exerting something akin to a superhuman effort, she managed to push all thoughts concerning Fernandez into a nether region, hoping that would free up the working part of her brain for more important things.

"You're staring at me," Esteban said abruptly just as the elevator arrived. The stainless-steel doors yawned open, temporarily awaiting their pleasure. "My shirt inside out or something?"

As he asked the question, he looked down to check himself out. Nothing appeared to be out of order to him, but he couldn't see the total picture.

"Your clothes are just fine," she told him, confident that he was already aware of that small fact.

His attitude might have sounded careless to the undiscerning ear, but her gut told her that Esteban Fernandez was far from a careless man. For one thing, he wouldn't have been able to survive in the world he'd previously chosen to descend into if he'd been cavalier by nature.

"I was just thinking that you clean up nicely," she finally told him.

Compliments, when they were intended for him rather than the persona he'd assumed these past three years, made Esteban uncomfortable. He had absolutely no idea how to accept them or what was expected from him by way of a response.

So he shrugged, trying to appear unfazed—something he had gotten exceedingly good at—and mumbled, "Thanks, you too."

To Kari's knowledge, yesterday she hadn't exactly looked like something the cat had dragged in—the way he most definitely had—but rather than begin a debate and possibly set him off, she decided to ignore the comment. "Okay. Moving on now."

They got out on the first floor, and she led the way to the rear of the building rather than to the front of it. The back was where the department vehicles were all kept parked.

"You okay with my driving?" she asked, turning toward him suddenly. At least one of her brothers and two of her old partners had never felt comfortable when she was behind the wheel. She came to the conclusion that they all had issues that had nothing to do with her. She, on the other hand, was secure enough to have someone else drive if that was what kept them happy.

"Why?" he asked suspiciously. "Something wrong with your driving?"

It amused her that *that* was the first thing that occurred to him. "No, it's just that most males prefer to be the ones behind the wheel."

He shrugged again. "Well, not this male. You're the one with the address, right?"

"Right." She was still just a tad wary of his motives. That it might just be a simple matter seemed *too* simple. For now, she reserved her judgment.

"So, you drive."

To him, it seemed like the logical, not to mention simple, approach. He only cared about being the one behind the wheel when he didn't trust the other people in the car.

But he wasn't part of that world anymore, he reminded himself for possibly the dozenth time since yesterday. Having someone else behind the wheel was the least of the things he was going to need to get accustomed to with this new job that had been thrust on him.

Provided he stuck around.

"Okay, then," Kari declared, pushing open one of the glass double doors and walking out. "The car's parked right over there."

Pointing for form's sake, she led the way down the steps and through the lot. Her route formed a rather zigzag pattern.

Esteban remained at her side, matching her step for step without offering a single word, like a tall, unobtrusive shadow.

That, Kari silently promised herself, was going to have to change.

And soon.

Chapter 5

"What the hell kept you?" were the first words out of the storage-utility manager's lips when Kari identified herself and her silent partner some fifteen minutes later.

There was a look of contempt on his pockmarked face as he eyed the IDs that were held up for him. "I was just about to use the bolt cutters on the lock and open the unit myself."

Rather than risk further undermining their authority by making excuses to the already hostile man, Kari deftly changed the subject, "Then you don't have keys to the unit?"

The manager—Alfred Jennings, according to the

sun-bleached stencil on the door of his closetlike office—looked annoyed that the female detective should even ask that question.

"Can't you read?" he demanded, every syllable dripping with sarcasm. "Didn't you see the words *Self-Storage* outside? That means the renter provides his or her own lock with its own key. Gives them privacy," he added with a condescending snort.

"It also costs you less if they provide their own lock," Esteban pointed out somberly. The manager began to scowl but confronted by the dark look on Esteban's face, he quickly backed off.

"Take us to the unit," she instructed. "And bring along your bolt cutters, please."

"Sure thing," Jennings bit off. Circumventing the two detectives, he got out in front of them and led the way to the storage unit in question, which was located at the rear of the facility.

Kari made a quick assessment of her surroundings as she and Esteban followed the manager.

At first glance, the facility looked like a mock-up movie set that had been abandoned before the designers could decide what it was supposed to look like. A haphazard collection of attached, short, single-story gray structures occupied the small lot.

At this hour of the morning, there were no other people about, taking inventory of their possessions or searching for that one elusive thing they were certain had to be in the storage unit because it hadn't shown up anywhere else. As Kari and her partner walked behind Jennings, a sickening, somewhat putrid smell started to become evident. Once noted, it seemed to swiftly increase in intensity.

There was no breeze this morning and, unimpeded, the smell seemed to fill up every square inch of available air, hovering over them like an ominous, thick cloud.

Fighting back a gagging reflex, Kari automatically covered her nose and mouth with her hand.

He'd stopped before the offending unit. "You see? You see what I mean?" Jennings demanded, his tone of voice bordering on hysteria. "It wasn't like this yesterday."

Kari sincerely doubted that, unless whatever it was that was causing this smell had been deposited in the unit sometime during the night. "Were you here yesterday?" she asked Jennings.

"No," he snapped, "but the guy who was here didn't say anything about this stink to me."

"He probably never left the office," Esteban theorized, his deep, monotone voice rumbling across the surface of the would-be dispute.

Surprised that Esteban had actually offered an opinion, Kari bit back the desire to cry out, "He speaks." She didn't have to be a genius to know that Fernandez would be less than thrilled to be teased in front of a third party, but she did flash him a look of feigned shock at the two cents he'd inserted into the verbal exchange.

The storage-utility manager said nothing in response. Instead, he muttered something under his breath that was surely less than flattering.

"This is it," Jennings said needlessly, gesturing toward the padlocked door of unit number 2041 as he choked out the words.

Kari nodded at the lock. "Go ahead, cut off the lock," she ordered, uttering the words on a single breath. She was struggling to inhale as little as possible. Jennings raised the bolt cutters he'd brought with him. Opening the jaws, his biceps shook as he applied the cutters to the lock.

The pressure he exerted was not enough. The lock remained intact. A second attempt was as futile as the first.

Disgusted, Kari was about to take the tool from Jennings and attempt to cut the lock herself when she found her way blocked. To her surprise, Esteban commandeered the tool with the authority of someone who was accustomed to having no opposition—and not tolerating any if he did.

Taking the bolt cutters in his big, manly hands, he opened the tool as far as it would go, securely fitted the cutting edge around the lock and, with one quick, reverberating snap of his forearms, cut the lock clean off.

Useless, the heavy metal object fell to the floor with a solid thud.

Stepping back from the defunct lock, Esteban handed the bolt cutters back to Jennings with one hand while raising up the dull red corrugated door with the other.

The putrid smell of something rotting had been strong before. Without the door in the way to mute it somewhat, it assaulted them with a one-two punch that was almost unbearable.

Kari could feel her eyes begin to sting and threaten to water. The sooner they got this over with, the better, she silently told herself.

But before she could make a move to try to hone in on the origin of the smell, Esteban strode into the small, cluttered rectangular unit ahead of her.

He used the daylight that was streaming in behind him as illumination to help him carefully look around.

Rather than say anything or make a guess at the source of the awful odor, Kari watched as Esteban made his way to the back, moving through the piles of cartons and boxes that stood between him and the far wall.

Reaching the back, he started to push aside the obstacles he encountered, working his way down to the bottom of an exceptionally large pile comprised of half a dozen different things that were indiscriminately tossed on top of one another. At the end of his search, Esteban found himself looking at what appeared to be a rolled-up Persian rug.

Appearing unfazed by the pungent odor, he looked over his shoulder at Kari.

"There's your smell," he concluded with finality, not even bothering to first investigate whether or not the rug actually contained anything.

He didn't have to.

He knew that smell, had come in contact with it more than once. Members of the cartel didn't consider an argument actually won until the opposing side was tucked away in a fashion closely resembling this one. The rugs they used weren't Persian, but the concept and execution were the same.

Not to be left out, Kari took it from there. She squatted down beside one end and, drawing in a deep breath that she fully intended to hold on to as long as humanly possible, she started to push aside as many layers of the rug as she feasibly could.

The unit was far too crowded for her to attempt to unfurl the rug—even if she could, which, at this point, she really couldn't. There were protocols to follow.

The rug was fairly stiff and it offered a lot of resistance, but she refused to be defeated and kept at it.

Standing back, Esteban watched her for a few moments, amused by her efforts as well as somewhat impressed by them. He let her continue for a little while, then put his hand over hers, a silent indication for her to stop.

"What are you doing?" she asked in confusion.

"Keeping you from wearing yourself out." With the

ease of someone who was accustomed to strong resistance, he completed the job that would have taken her three times as long to finish—if at all. He pushed aside enough of the rug to expose what was housed inside. They were both looking down at an older, gray-haired man, who from all indications, had to have been dead for at least several days. Possibly even a week.

Eager to see just how ghoulish this sight actually was, the storage-facility manager pushed his way forward to get a better look at who—or what—was wrapped up in the rug.

When he saw who it was, his eagerness instantly faded. "Oh, hell," he moaned. "I know him."

Kari looked at Jennings, her interest piqued. "Who is he?" she wanted to know.

He frowned, but this time the frown was because of the situation, not because of her or her partner. "Don't remember his name offhand, but that's the guy who rents the unit."

It was Kari's turn to frown. "Congratulations, Fernandez."

"For what?" he wanted to know.

"On the job less than two hours and you've already caught your first homicide," she told him.

Esteban said nothing in acknowledgment of the dubious so-called "honor." Instead, she saw him begin to clear away the piles of boxes and other various possessions that were surrounding the rug.

Kari shifted so that she managed to block his access to the closest pile of clutter. "Hold it," she cried. "What are you doing?"

He would have thought that was self-evident, but maybe she wasn't as savvy as he'd thought. "Pushing things aside so that we can unfurl this damn rug and take a closer look at the victim."

But as he turned to get back to what he was doing, Kari caught his arm by the sleeve and tried to hold him back. Even though she'd managed to catch him off guard, holding his arm still took more effort than she'd anticipated.

"You can't do that," she told him.

The look he gave her clearly said he thought she'd lost her mind. "Why not?"

Rather than answer him, Kari glanced at Jennings. The storage-facility manager looked as if he had become one giant set of ears.

"You can go now," she said, dismissing the man. "We'll call you if we need anything else."

"I got no place else to be," Jennings said, remaining firmly planted where he was and intently staring at the rolled-up rug.

"Yes," she informed him firmly, "you do."

The man's squinty eyes narrowed even more. "Where?" he challenged.

"Anywhere but here." Kari's tone left no room for argument. Having no choice, Jennings was forced to withdraw, and she heard him grumbling to himself as he stomped away.

Kari waited until the man was completely out of the storage unit before she turned back to look at Esteban. He was still waiting for his answer.

"We have to wait for the CSI unit to get here and process this crime scene before we can actually touch anything in it."

Following protocol, she knew that she shouldn't have even pulled back the rug the way she had, but if she hadn't, they wouldn't have been able to actually label this a crime scene, so she supposed she could be forgiven in that instance.

After three years of living solely by his wits and going with gut instincts, Esteban was accustomed to following his own rules. By-the-book procedure was something he vaguely remembered coming across at the academy, but he hadn't ever followed that in the field. It didn't really make much sense, especially not when it came to dealing with life-or-death situations.

"You mean we just have to sit here and cool our heels?" he asked impatiently.

She nodded her head. "That's just how it's done." She didn't like it any more than he did, but she liked having cases thrown out of court even less, especially when she busted her tail to put the cases together in the first place.

He snorted dismissively. The look on his face was *not* impassive at the moment, and it told her exactly what he thought of how "things were done."

"Not in my world," he responded.

"But we're not in your world anymore," she informed him, making the best of an irritating situation. "We're in mine. And in case you think you can argue me out of following proper procedure, I think you should know that my dad's the head of the CSI day unit."

She couldn't quite fathom the look he gave her, but it definitely didn't even remotely fit under the heading of agreeable.

Or even resigned.

"Of course he is," Esteban responded curtly. Looking down at the hold she still had on the cuff of his shirt, he said, "You can let go now."

No, I can't, not yet, she thought.

She continued clutching his sleeve. "And I can trust you to back away from the body and just wait for the unit to arrive?"

He didn't like it, but he'd do it. He'd had enough friction for the time being.

Shrugging, he told her, "Pay's the same whether I wait or not, so yeah, you can trust me to back away from the body and wait for the crime unit to come with their cameras to take their pretty pictures—even if the whole thing's dumb."

Kari let go of his shirtsleeve, dropping her hand to her side.

"It's only dumb," she corrected him, "when you see the case you've toiled tirelessly over being thrown out of court because one stupid misstep has crucial evidence being ruled inadmissible." Her head was beginning to ache from the smell assaulting her. "Off the record, I agree with you, but that's just the way things are."

She'd managed to mildly spark his interest—besides, he had to do something while waiting, and asking questions was as good a way as any to pass the time.

"It happened to you?" he asked, then clarified when she gave him a quizzical look. "Having something thrown out as inadmissible?"

She nodded. "Oh, yeah, it happened to me." And no amount of appealing to just about everyone she could think of had changed that. Taking out her cell phone, she pressed one preprogrammed number on the keypad, then waited as the phone on the other end rang. She silently counted off the rings, getting up to three. When the fourth ring came, she knew she was being connected to voice mail and sighed with displeasure because she hated talking to machines. But just as the fourth ring was fading, clearing a path for the robotic voice that was about to ask her to "please leave a message at the tone," Kari heard the cell being picked up on the other end.

And then a deep voice announced, "Crime lab, Cavanaugh."

Her father had taken to his new/old name like a duck to water, she thought. All those years of feeling as if he wasn't quite in sync with the rest of his family finally made sense now. They, the Cavellis, really *hadn't* been the rest of his family.

At least, not in total.

He was a Cavanaugh no matter what his birth certificate had initially stated. She was just glad for his sake that the error had finally come to light, giving him the opportunity to claim his birthright if he wanted it.

"Hi, Dad," she said without bothering to announce herself. "I'm in need of your stunningly focused expertise."

There wasn't even a second's hesitation on the other end of the call. A hearty laugh was immediately followed by, "Ah, Kari, my most perceptive offspring. You have a crime scene for me."

It wasn't a guess but a statement of fact. With rare insight, Sean Cavanaugh knew each of his children inside out.

"All but gift-wrapped," she told him. "My new partner and I found a dead body wrapped up in what looks like an old Persian rug. Rug and body are currently stashed in a storage facility on Edinger and East Yale Loop. I need you and your team of roving experts to process the crime scene for me so I can get on with the case."

"Address?" he asked. She rattled it off for him, having already committed it to memory. "All right, Kari, the team and I will be there as soon as I finish up here," he promised.

So, he'd already scored another crime scene. There was a time, according to the stories her father had told them, that the only crime in Aurora revolved around littering.

"Busy morning?" she murmured.

"Too busy," he answered. But he wasn't one to go on about his work, so he said, "Be there as soon as we can," and then terminated the call.

"How long?" Esteban wanted to know the moment Kari returned her cell phone to her pocket and headed back to him.

Sugarcoating it got her no extra points and she knew it. So she went with the truth.

"Not sure," she confessed.

Esteban was already growing impatient, and they were still within their first fifteen minutes at the crime scene.

"And we're just supposed to stand here, staring off into space until they get here?" he groused.

"You can handle the staring part if you want," she told him glibly. "I'm going to go and see what I can get out of that manager guy. He struck me as someone who liked sticking his nose into everyone's business. Maybe we can get that to work for us," she said as she walked out of the storage unit.

The second she did, her eyes stopped stinging. She wondered how big a job it was to disinfect an entire storage unit. Jennings was not going to be a happy camper, she couldn't help thinking.

The all but silent footfall behind her meant that her partner had opted to leave the storage unit, as well. It came as no surprise.

Obviously, Mr. Macho's had enough of this smell, too, she thought, amused.

Chapter 6

When she and Esteban strolled into the small office where the manager of the storage facility spent most of his time, Jennings was already at his desk, hunched over his computer.

The staccato sound of keys being struck in less than a rhythmic fashion told her that the poor typist was either busy spreading the word that his storage facility had been the scene of a gruesome murder, or he was searching through old records to see if he could uncover anything about the poor old sap who had been renting the unit. Jennings suddenly looked up, startled, when the sound of the door slamming shut—thanks to a gust of wind—reverberated through the dust-laden office.

Surprise swiftly turned into annoyance. "You're still here," he complained.

"Yes, we are," Kari acknowledged, deliberately sounding cheerful. She could tell that irritated him, which seemed only fair since Jennings's noncompliant attitude irritated *her.* "I see you've had a chance to look up the deceased's name."

Kari actually couldn't "see" anything of the kind, but she surmised that it would have been the manager's first order of business the second he got back into his cubbyhole of an office. The flushed expression on his face told her she'd guessed right.

"What is it?" she asked him, her eyes all but nailing him to his chair.

Jennings squirmed uncomfortably. He evidently didn't like being read like a book. "William Reynolds," he answered, not without a trace of reluctance.

"And what's the late Mr. Reynolds's address?" she wanted to know.

A nervously defiant look came over his face. "That's confidential," Jennings informed her. "I can't go around giving out our customers' addresses."

Esteban leaned over the thin, gouged beige counter that separated the man's office from the small space in front of the outer door.

"We're not asking for 'addresses,' we're asking for *an* address," he told the manager, "and the information's not 'confidential' unless you're a priest and it was given to you while taking Reynolds's confession."

Esteban spoke softly, but each word he uttered carried weight and, strung together, they came very close to sounding as if there was a threat waiting in the wings.

Beginning to sweat, Jennings sucked in his breath and then hit a series of keys on the keyboard.

"There!" he declared, gesturing at the screen. "Satisfied?" His derisive question was intended for both of the detectives who'd so vexingly invaded his minor domain.

Kari raised her cell phone and took a quick picture of the information on the monitor. She caught the quizzical look on her partner's face.

"It beats writing," she told him. "Besides, I've got pretty terrible handwriting," she added.

It was the kind that, unless she actually remembered what it was that she'd jotted down earlier, she had difficulty deciphering.

"You should work on that," Esteban commented.

Maybe she liked him better when he didn't talk, she thought, not quite sure if he was being serious or sarcastic. In either case, she didn't welcome the unsolicited advice.

Turning her attention back to the less than cooperative storage-facility manager, she asked one final question. "Is there anything you can tell us about the deceased?"

Jennings was still guarded. "Like what?" he replied.

She couldn't decide if the man was hiding something or was just uncooperative with the law in general. "Like did you hear him arguing with anyone? Did he look upset in the last week or so?"

He raised and lowered his shoulders in a vague, dismissive manner. "I only saw him maybe a couple of times."

"Recently?" Esteban growled out the word, issuing it like a challenge.

"N-no," Jennings stammered, clearly uncomfortable when Esteban addressed him. The manager thought for a moment, then said, "He paid his bill on time and never gave me any trouble."

She supposed that was something—or a *non-*something. Nonetheless, she said thank-you as she took out one of her business cards. "If you do happen to think of something else, you can reach me at this number." She placed the card on his desk.

Jennings picked it up and looked down at the number imprinted on the face of the off-white business card. "If I call this number, I'll just get you?" he asked, raising one eyebrow as he looked up at her.

There was no way she was going to have the man thinking this was about anything but the murder. "That's the precinct number for both of us," she informed him in a clipped voice.

"Oh." Suddenly disinterested, Jennings tossed the card onto the side of the desk just as they began to walk out.

"Looks like you just blew your chances for a date,"

Esteban quipped. The smallest hint of a grin accompanied his wry observation.

Kari narrowed her eyes at him as she banked down her surprise. "You have a sense of humor. Reassuring," she commented. "As for your remark, I'd rather eat dirt."

If he was going to comment on her unappetizing choice of entrée, the words died unspoken as both he and Kari saw the Aurora Police Department's white CSI van pull up onto the storage facility's grounds.

"That way," Kari called out to the driver, who was none other than her father. She pointed in the general direction of Reynolds's storage unit.

Rather than say anything, Sean Cavanaugh briefly stuck his hand out the driver's-side window and gave a quick wave in response before continuing on his way. Kari followed quickly behind the vehicle.

She didn't bother looking over her shoulder to see if Fernandez had opted to wait for her in the car or to follow her lead.

Now that the scene was going to be thoroughly documented, she wanted to get at the body wrapped up in the rug. There could be something on the torso that could help them figure out who killed Reynolds and why.

Sean Cavanaugh and his two investigators were already inside the storage unit when she reached it. The sound of cameras clicking, freezing the crime scene in time, greeted her as she walked in.

One thing struck her immediately. The smell was just as appalling the second time around as it had been the first.

"Drumming up business for my department?" her father asked as he snapped another picture of the rug and the victim within it.

"Actually, I thought I'd make my new partner's first day on the job an unforgettable one," she jested.

"New partner," Sean repeated. This was the first he'd heard about Kari getting someone new to work with. "That would be you?" he asked, looking over his daughter's head at the tall and striking dark-haired man who was half a step behind her.

Kari turned around. Damn, but he was incredibly quiet, she thought for a second time. He didn't seem to make a sound when he moved. If he stayed on, she might have to give serious consideration to getting him a bell to wear around his neck.

"So you did decide to come along," she murmured.

Esteban ignored her for the time being, looking instead at the man who'd asked him a question.

"Detective Esteban Fernandez," he said, extending his hand to the man he assumed was the supervisor of the CSI day crew. He had a very authoritative manner about him that lent itself well to the position.

"Sean Cavanaugh," Sean introduced himself, taking the offered hand in his.

The younger man had a good, solid handshake, Sean thought. You could tell a great deal about a man by the way he stepped up and presented himself. He felt a little more at ease about his daughter being out in the field. This partner, he judged, would have her back.

"My daughter giving you a hard time?" he asked Esteban amicably.

"Not that I noticed, sir," the detective replied with stoic resignation that was not wasted on Sean. He took a second look at the young man, and then looked at his daughter. *This could prove to be interesting,* Sean thought.

Kari noted the subtle shift, but before she could say anything, one of her father's two assistants called out to him.

"Sean, come look at this," Destiny Richardson requested. She and the other investigator had managed to carefully unfurl and remove the rug from around the victim's body. The entire area where the rug had been in direct contact with the dead man was completely soaked with blood.

Kari was right beside her father and looked down at the corpse sans his cocoon. "Looks like he was killed on that rug," she theorized.

"Or wrapped up immediately after he was killed," Esteban interjected. Inherent concern masked by a veil of curiosity had him glancing in her direction to see how she was handling this up-close view of murder. That her pallor hadn't changed nor had she bolted to purge her suddenly nauseated stomach, drew grudging admiration from him. "Looks like cause of death was having his throat slashed," Esteban observed.

"At least it was quick," Kari said, then raised her eyes up to her father's, looking for confirmation. "It was quick, right?"

Sean nodded. "That would be my preliminary guess, at least for now. I'll know more once we get him back to the lab."

"How long do you think he's been dead?" Kari asked.

Rather than answer, Sean looked at the investigator who had called him over to the unveiled body. Destiny, the young woman he had initially taken under his wing and personally trained because she had such an aptitude for the work, was soon going to become an official member of the family. She was engaged to Kari's older brother, Logan.

Right now, though, she had just removed the thermometer she'd inserted into the victim's liver in order to ascertain body temperature, which in turn allowed them to establish approximate time of death.

"According to his liver temperature, I'd say that he's been dead close to a week," Destiny estimated.

"You heard the lady," Sean said to his daughter.

Before she could thank Destiny, Esteban was calling her attention to something else.

"Hey, Hyphen," he said, using the same nickname that he'd heard the lieutenant use.

Kari looked in his direction, not entirely sure if she

liked the man calling her that or not. She supposed it beat Fernandez referring to her as "hey, you," so for now she let it go.

"Yes?" she responded, waiting.

"What do you make of this?" While the others were gathered around the victim's head, looking at him upside down, Esteban was standing on the other end of the body, peering down at the victim's chest.

Kari circumvented the body, coming over to stand next to her partner. "Make of what?" she wanted to know.

"This." Esteban pointed to the front of the dead man's pullover sport shirt.

She squinted, trying to see exactly what it was that had caught her partner's eye, other than the massive bloodstain that had soaked through the entire front of what looked to have been a light green shirt. The deceased had a large neck, and all three buttons at his neckline were open.

She didn't notice anything until she looked down a second time. Staring at the shirt, she began to make out what looked like a crude drawing that had been stenciled in with a black laundry marker.

A message from the killer?

"If I had to make a wild guess, I'd say that looks like the scales of justice."

She looked up at her partner, waiting to hear if he concurred with her or made out some other kind of symbol. The drawing looked almost primitive, but if it had indeed been left by the killer, maybe he'd been interrupted before he could finish his artwork.

Rather than agree or disagree with her guess, Esteban looked over to the head of the crime lab for his assessment. "Chief?"

Sean studied the stained drawing for a moment. "Scales of justice gets my vote. Whoever did that definitely needs to brush up on their technique," he added.

"Let's hope he does it on a canvas and not a person," Kari quipped. "Let me—let *us,*" she corrected herself, not wanting her new partner to think she was trying to slight him, "know if you find out anything interesting in the autopsy."

She'd stopped herself just short of saying "Dad" at the end of her request. For the most part, she kept her professional life separate from her private one, but there were times when it was far too easy just to slip up when she was dealing with her family.

And now it had become that much more difficult with the vast increase of family members.

Sean nodded absently in response, his mind already moving on to another part of the procedure. But just as Kari began to leave the storage unit, he remembered to remind her about something.

"See you Sunday," he called out.

Walking quickly out of the unit in an effort to once again leave the awful smell behind, she caught herself waiting for Esteban to ask about the reminder. When he didn't, she decided that her new partner didn't possess a shred of normal curiosity.

She decided to volunteer the information anyway. "He means Sunday dinner."

Esteban merely nodded. "I kind of figured," he said offhandedly.

She knew someone else would have just dropped it, but someone else most likely wouldn't mind dealing with the silent treatment. She, however, did. Habitual silences had always been an indication of awkwardness as far as she as concerned. And if you felt awkward around someone, you definitely didn't feel as if they had your six, which in turn went to trust. Trust, she had found, even in her young career, was the most important part of police work. If you didn't have trust, you didn't have confidence…and if you didn't have confidence, you were nothing more than a walking target, waiting to be taken down.

"Seems that the former chief of police, Andrew Cavanaugh—now one of my two brand-new uncles—likes to have the family over on Sundays. He goes all out—cooks a huge meal. He throws his doors open to welcome as much of the family as can turn up.

"And I hear that when *everyone* shows up, there're too many people to fit into the house all at the same time." She looked at her partner as they reached the car. He hadn't so much as grunted in response to what she'd just said. "You're not listening to any of this, are you?" As far as she was concerned, it was really a rhetorical question.

Rather than answer yes or no, Esteban had a question of his own.

"Would it matter?" he asked her. "You seem to like to talk, and I've got a pulse." He looked at her over the hood of the car before getting in. "I figure that's about all you require."

Kari got in behind the steering wheel and buckled up, snapping the metal tongue into the slot. "You are a cynical son of a gun, aren't you?"

"What I am, Hyphen, is a survivor," Esteban told her.

Kari put the key into the ignition and left it there for the time being. "Is that what you're doing?" she wanted to know. "Trying to survive this partnership?"

Esteban didn't answer. He assumed that if he let enough time pass, she'd forget about it. But then something told him this wasn't going to be the case here.

He could feel Kari's eyes staring at him. Could *feel* her waiting. She hadn't started up the vehicle yet and something told him that she wouldn't, not until he made some sort of a response.

"If you're going to require answers and input each and every time, then I'm going to have to rethink this whole association," he told her matter-of-factly.

Kari sighed. She couldn't just wait him out. They had to get going.

"We'll work on it," she promised, then, for his benefit, she decided to lapse into silence for a while, at least until they reached the dead man's apartment.

The trip took all of ten minutes.

Getting out of the car, she spared Esteban a look. "Quiet enough for you?"

He looked somewhat disappointed that the solitude had been broken so soon.

"It was," he replied. "But I guess all good things must come to an end."

"At least for now." Then she couldn't resist adding, "I doubt if Reynolds's neighbors would appreciate my asking them questions using hand puppets."

The picture that evoked in his mind made him laugh. It was a deep, rich sound that seemed to immediately weave directly under her skin.

She didn't need this, she thought.

"You never know," Esteban quipped, "it might be worth a shot."

"I'll keep it in mind as a last resort," she said dryly, doing her best to ignore his effect on her. He wasn't irritating her in the least, just unsettling her.

Pausing just short of the building superintendent's door, Kari looked over to Esteban just before she rang the doorbell.

"I'll do the talking," she told him, intending to relieve him of the pressure of actually having to form words.

She was about to tell him as much when she heard him say, "I figured you would."

"Nice to know I haven't disappointed you," she said to him.

She wasn't sure, but she could have sworn that he said, "Yet," under his breath.

It was all the challenge she needed.

Chapter 7

"Murdered, you say," the building superintendent, Walter Meyers, said for a third time as he shook his bald head.

It was obvious that he was having trouble wrapping his mind around the concept. The barrel-chested older man had insisted on coming along with them to unlock the late William Reynolds's fifth-floor apartment.

"You sure it was murder?" he asked Esteban. Putting the key in the lock, he twisted it and opened the door, but blocked it with his rather wide body.

Esteban deliberately moved the overall-clad, heavy-set superintendent out of the way. "Most people don't enclose themselves up in a rug, then slit their own throats," he deadpanned as he and Kari walked into the apartment.

Inside it smelled stagnant and oppressive.

This place sure could use some ventilation, Kari thought to herself as she slipped on a pair of plastic gloves. Since Esteban was not following suit, she dug into her pocket and produced a second pair. She wordlessly held them out to him.

After a beat, Esteban took them from her and slid the gloves on.

Satisfied, Kari turned to Meyers. "What can you tell us about Mr. Reynolds?" she asked. "Did he get into arguments with his neighbors or have any enemies that you're aware of?"

She left it open-ended, waiting for the superintendent to fill in the details.

He shrugged his wide, squat shoulders in response to her question. "Far as I know, everyone liked the guy. He wasn't that much of a talker, especially after his wife passed on, but he always had a friendly word to offer if you ran into him in the elevator. Paid his rent on time, never made any demands or had any complaints."

"Where did he work?" Kari asked. Out of the corner of her eye, she saw that her partner was already carefully going over the small apartment, looking for signs of a struggle that would indicate that the victim had been killed here. By his expression, she gath-

ered that Reynolds had most likely met his end somewhere else.

"He didn't," Meyers was telling her. "He was retired from the post office. He mentioned doing some
volunteer work at the local hospital. Said he didn't
like rattling around the apartment now that his wife
was gone." He shook his head as if he couldn't fathom
the notion. "Me, I'd be thrilled to death to be able to
just bum around the apartment without having my
wife breathing down my neck." The superintendent
sounded almost wistful.

Kari had no doubt that the woman in question
would probably say the same thing about him, given
half a chance. It made her wonder how some couples
ever wound up with each other.

She caught herself looking at Esteban as she pondered that. The next moment, she deliberately looked
away. "Would you happen to know which hospital?"
she asked Meyers.

He shook his head. "Sorry—he never said. Just that
on a good day he could get there on foot."

Well, that certainly narrows it down, Kari thought.
*After all, what are the odds that there's more than one
hospital in the area within walking distance?*

"Hey, Hyphen," Esteban called to her. "Come look
at this."

She saw that look of curiosity flicker in Meyers's
eyes. However, she was *not* about to enlighten the
stranger about her deplorable nickname.

Instead, she told the man, "Thanks. If we need anything else, I'll be sure to let you know."

Meyers dug in his heels. "That's okay…I can hang around for a while," he told her, craning his neck to see what it was that the other detective had found.

Some people, Kari decided, had to be beaten over the head before they took the hint.

"No, you can't," Kari informed him with a smile. "We'll take it from here." She left no room for argument, although Meyers did look as if he really wanted to convince her to let him stay.

But after a moment, the man sighed and retreated.

Only once the man was out of the apartment did she turn to go and find her partner. But by then, Esteban had evidently grown tired of waiting and had returned to the living room to show her what he'd found.

He was carrying a small black binder that looked as if it had seen years of wear and tear. When he came closer, she saw that the spine appeared to be slightly cracked down the middle.

"Find a secret diary?" she asked, only half joking.

On the job only a few years, she'd learned not to be surprised by anything. The man thought to be a saint could very easily turn out to be a sinner of the highest caliber.

But not today, she learned as Esteban answered her question.

"No, I found his address book." He held it out to

her. "From the faded ink and coffee stains on it, I'd say it's probably a few decades old, if not more."

She took the book from him and perused a few pages. "A lot of the entries are crossed out," she noticed, then raised her eyes to Esteban's. "People he's not speaking to anymore?"

"Or people who've moved or died" came Esteban's reply.

Kari thumbed through a few more pages, then threw out a few far-out ideas. "Maybe he 'helped' those people to die. His murder could be someone's idea of payback—or justice," she pointed out. "That could explain the crude drawing of the scales of justice on his shirt."

Esteban inclined his head. "It's possible," he allowed, although he didn't look all that convinced. Taking back the book, he picked up where she'd left off paging through it. "Looks like he's got a relative in New York. A Sandra Reynolds."

"Could be a daughter or a sister," she speculated. "If Reynolds worked for the post office, we can get next of kin information from them. Nice work," she commented, nodding at the address book.

Rather than welcome the compliment, Esteban shot her a derisive look. "I don't need to be patted on my head like an overeager, wet-behind-the-ears recruit every time I do something you approve of."

Wow, she thought. *That's some chip you have on your shoulder.*

"Fine," she told him out loud. "Next time I'll just hit you with a stick." She tucked the book into her over-size purse, planning to go through it more thoroughly once she had it logged in as evidence. "Meanwhile, I thought we'd go pay Little Sisters of Mercy a call."

He maintained an apartment here, but it had been years since he'd lived in the area. The terrain, which had undergone changes, was somewhat unfamiliar to him now.

"You mean the hospital?" he asked, trying to place a location in his mind.

"No, the strip club," she quipped. "Of course the hospital. From what I could ascertain from Meyers, our dead former mail carrier volunteered there. Maybe hospital personnel could enlighten us about any rela-tionships he had that might have caused him to wind up being gift-wrapped in a rug."

"Worth a try." Esteban gestured for her to lead the way out of the apartment. "You're the one driving," he reminded her.

It almost sounded to her as if he didn't *want* to get behind the wheel. That didn't jibe with the macho image she recalled, so she decided to bait him just a little.

"Yes, but I'm not a fanatic about it. Anytime you want to relieve me and drive for a while, just say the word."

When he looked over at her, she had the impression that he'd guessed at her elementary strategy.

"I've got no problem with you driving," he informed her mildly.

Yes, but I have a problem with you not having a problem, she mused to herself, heading toward the elevator.

Patty Simon, the older woman in charge of keeping track and scheduling the hospital's volunteers, looked somewhat leery when they asked about William Reynolds's work history. As it turned out, she was a self-professed procedural-TV junky who had logged in hundreds of hours watching every program devoted even in some minor way to the field of forensic science. Patty initially answered all their questions without incident, but then she suddenly burst into tears midway through the interview.

"Something happened to him, didn't it?" Patty cried, figuring out the reason behind all the veiled questions about William Reynolds.

Her interest instantly piqued—this could all be an elaborate performance—Kari asked, "What makes you say that?"

Instead of a direct answer, Patty sobbed, "It's all my fault. *My* fault."

Kari exchanged looks with Esteban. Could it be this easy? She sincerely doubted it, but sometimes the gods did smile down on poor, hardworking detectives.

"Go on," Kari coaxed the woman. "Why is it your fault?"

"Then he *is* dead," Patty lamented. Fresh tears slid down her rounded cheeks. "It's my fault because he'd finally asked me out. We were going to that new restaurant on Von Karmen this Friday." Rolling her eyes heavenward, she made no effort to stifle her sobs. "I have the *worst* luck with men. The last man who asked me out was in this awful car wreck. And another man canceled his date with me because he was suddenly facing a major audit by the IRS."

Stifling a hiccup, Patty dug into the pocket of her pink smock and pulled out a crumpled tissue. She used it to wipe her eyes. "I'm like Typhoid Mary. I've got to find a way to discourage men from asking me out…."

From where she was standing, the older woman did *not* appear to be a femme fatale. It really did take all kinds, Kari thought.

"You work on that," she told the other woman. "Meanwhile, is there anything you can tell us about Mr. Reynolds?"

"Only that he was a sweet, wonderful man who always had a smile. Can you tell me what happened to him?" she asked, her eyes all but eagerly begging for details. She looked from her to Esteban, hoping one of them would tell her.

"I'm afraid not," Kari said gently. "We can't give out any details on an ongoing investigation."

There was desperation in the woman's deep-set brown eyes. "But he is dead?"

With all her heart, Kari wished it wasn't so, not just for Patty Simon's sake, but mostly for Reynolds's sake.

"Yes, very," she told the older woman.

Patty sighed. Her tears drying, she got back down to business. "I'm going to have to find someone to fill in William's spot on Thursday," she said. "It won't be easy," she confided.

"Then we'll leave you to your work," Kari said. Handing the woman her card, as she'd done with the others, Kari encouraged her to call if she remembered any further details.

"Everyone you deal with that crazy?" Esteban asked her after they had left the hospital's main lobby and were headed back to where they had parked the car. "A man's dead and all that woman thinks about is her own bad luck. *Her* bad luck?" he questioned incredulously. "What the hell about Reynolds's luck? Or is that just considered collateral damage?"

Kari paused to flash him an amused grin over the roof of the car. "Welcome to the wonderful world of homicide," she cracked.

She was about to get into the vehicle when her cell phone rang.

"Cavelli-Cavanaugh," she answered briskly. It was obvious from her expression that she was unhappy with whatever was being said, and he felt a rush of adrenaline course through his veins in anticipation of what was to come.

"Yes, we'll be right there," Kari told the person on

the other end of the line before terminating the call. The connection broken, she slipped the phone back into her pocket.

"Let me guess," Esteban said. "It's *not* good news."

"That's putting it mildly," she told him. "We can stop looking at the case as an isolated incident…."

It wasn't hard to guess why she looked like that. "Another body?"

"Another body," she repeated heavily.

Esteban's expression remained unchanged, and he asked for street directions wearing that same impenetrable look. All of a sudden, she felt a growing need to somehow break through that outer shell of his, to reach the part of him she was certain could still feel. After all, it had been inside him once—why not still?

"Same M.O.?" he asked her.

She considered that point. "Yes and no. The location is different, but the woman's throat was slashed just like our retired mail carrier's was—and she's a retired teacher."

Two retired victims in a row. Esteban frowned. He doubted if that was just a coincidence in the killer's random selection process.

"Maybe someone's got it in for retired people," he cracked.

"Terrific," Kari retorted, sincerely hoping that was *not* the case. "Then we're going to need a hell of a lot bigger task force," she concluded, paraphrasing a famous line from a classic movie. Except in that case, the word "bigger" referred to acquiring a boat—this meant more manpower, something the department always seemed to be short of these days.

Esteban proceeded slowly, going over the facts of the first case and seeing if they measured up to the evidence in the second one.

"They didn't find the victim rolled up in a rug in a storage unit, did they?" Because that, he couldn't help thinking, would have been truly bizarre.

"No, no rug," Kari told him. "The victim's granddaughter hadn't heard from her for a few days, and when she tried to reach her, she didn't get an answer. She said that raised a red flag since her grandmother was always very good about returning calls. So the woman went to her grandmother's house to check up on her and found her in the kitchen, her throat slashed."

Esteban nodded as he took the new information in. "Maybe it's just a coincidence."

Kari slanted him a look as she eased her foot off the gas pedal and onto the brake, coming to a stop at a red light. That was overly optimistic, especially for him.

"You really think so?" she wanted to know.

He shook his head. "No."

She sighed. "Me neither. But I really don't like where this is headed." It had all the signs of a serial murder case in the making.

"Makes two of us," he commented brusquely.

* * *

The woman's granddaughter, Anne Daniels, had to be sedated and wasn't up to answering any questions by the time Kari and her partner reached the crime scene.

The cheery-looking town-house kitchen, bathed in afternoon sunlight, looked like an improbable place for a murder. But then, she'd learned that murder never cared about its surroundings. It barged in everywhere.

"I guess there's no question about where the victim was murdered," Esteban said grimly as he bent down to study the rather frail-looking dead woman. "There're no defensive wounds."

"He came up behind her and caught her by surprise." Kari let out a shaky breath. "The poor thing never had a chance. She looks like she could have been overpowered by a strong three-year-old."

"Notice anything else?" Esteban asked her.

She looked down at the body, wondering what he was referring to. "I'm not sure…" Then she glanced over at an eight-by-eleven cookie sheet. It was covered in parchment paper and a dozen extralarge mounds of cookie dough ready for the oven. "Baking cookies." She looked up at Esteban. "I think she was comfortable with whoever it was who killed her."

"Maybe," Esteban allowed. "Or maybe she was too busy to hear the intruder coming in. But I'm referring to what's missing."

Her eyes swept over the victim again. "Missing?"

He nodded. "No crude drawing of the scales of justice."

The story of Reynolds's murder had just hit the news, but the detail about the scales had been deliberately left out. "Maybe this is a copycat killer," she theorized.

"Maybe," he echoed in that stoic voice she was really starting to dislike.

Feeling frustrated, wanting to glean something useful, Kari went outside the town house and proceeded to question the neighbors, asking the standard questions about noise and any odd behavior. No one had seen or heard anything out of the ordinary.

"Batting zero here," Kari muttered, growing more exasperated.

Neighbors on both sides of the victim's town house were appalled that something like this could have happened to "such a lovely woman like Mae."

The two neighbors, a divorced vet and an unemployed construction worker who was currently in between significant others, had nothing but kind words about the woman, who'd periodically baked "the best damn raisin cookies on the planet" for the two men. Neither had heard any loud noises coming out of the woman's home.

"I wish I had. I wouldn't have let anything happen to Mae if only I'd known. She didn't deserve this," the construction worker—a large, burly man who gave Kari the impression of towering over her, even though he was the exact same height—said with genuine sorrow in his voice. "She wasn't…wasn't…you know." He stumbled over his words, then looked toward Esteban to fill in the missing term he couldn't make himself utter.

"No, she wasn't," Esteban answered, assuming that the man was asking whether the retired schoolteacher had been raped or violated in any way. "The M.E.'s preliminary exam indicated that she hadn't been violated." It was a lie. The M.E. hadn't even arrived yet, but the man asking looked really distressed, and Esteban felt for him. "Why?" he asked. "Do you know anyone who would—"

Esteban didn't get a chance to finish. The construction worker was shaking his head. "No, no, it's just that there're so many crazy people running around these days…. It's bad enough she was killed, but to have that happen first, well it's just unthinkable."

"From all appearances, it was quick," Esteban reassured him.

When both neighbors offered their services to "get justice for Mae," Kari quickly promised to let them know if there was any way they could help.

"Well, that was enlightening," she commented to her new partner as they walked away from the two men and headed back toward the victim's town house.

Esteban looked at her. A slight scowl formed on his

brow. Had he missed something? "You pick up something from what was said?"

"No. I meant enlightening about you," she corrected, glancing his way.

Esteban's frown deepened. She'd lost him. As far as he knew, he hadn't said anything of consequence. "What's that supposed to mean?"

"It means I didn't realize until just now that you still have a compassionate bone in your body. What you just said to that construction worker was meant to make him feel better. You and I both know that we won't get the whole story until the M.E. files his report." She smiled up at him. "So that was really nice of you. I would have bet money that you would have just walked away, leaving him to think the worst."

Esteban's intense blue eyes narrowed just as the CSI van turned the corner at the end of the block and drew closer. But he wasn't looking at the van—he was looking at Kari.

"What do you mean 'still'?" he wanted to know. Tossing out that word meant that she must have believed that he was compassionate before, and for that to be true, she had to have known him previously.

That, in turn, spoke to the vague feeling of familiarity he'd experienced in the Chief of Detectives' office.

The feeling, he realized, he was experiencing again now.

Plus more.

Esteban waited for her to answer him so he could put that sentiment to rest once and for all.

Chapter 8

Kari was trying to decide how best to frame her answer to her new partner's question when the CSI van pulled up in front of the latest victim's town house. For a moment, curious as to which of the team had come out to process this crime scene, she forgot about Fernandez.

The three team members quickly got out of the van. They lost no time arming themselves with the equipment needed to document any and all findings at the crime scene. After all, you never knew what could eventually give them that one clue that would help lead to the woman's killer.

Kari was surprised to see that her father was once

again heading up the team. She'd just assumed that he would still be focused on the last murder victim.

"Spreading yourself a little thin, aren't you, Dad?" Kari asked as she came up behind her father.

Sean closed the trunk and turned around to face her. "I could say the same thing to you and your partner here," he said, nodding at Esteban.

The latter returned the nod in kind, but refrained from saying anything.

"Not the same thing," Kari pointed out. "We caught the case because it looks like it might be the work of the same guy who killed our retired mail carrier."

"Actually, that's why I'm here, too." Picking up a case with one hand, a camera with the other, he strode toward the town-house door. A patrolman stood guarding it. "You know I can't resist serial killer cases," Sean said. "The sooner we can catch this killer and bring him—or her—in, the safer the public will be."

It wasn't anything that she hadn't heard before. Her father firmly believed that while a common killer might have been motivated by the heat of the moment, a serial killer had a blood lust that was never satisfied.

However, of late, seeing the bodies of the two slaughtered retirees had somehow made it seem more personal. Her father was years away from considering retirement—she had a feeling that he intended to die with his lab coat on, processing a case—but these victims were closer to his age bracket and it made her look at him in a whole new light.

It made her want to protect him, even though she knew she couldn't.

"Just don't go poking around in dangerous places," she cautioned.

Sean's smile was warm and understanding. She wasn't anywhere that he hadn't been himself, time and again, whenever he watched one of his own go out to answer a call.

"I could say the same thing to you," he reminded her. "And I've got the feeling that the warning would make about as much of an impression on you as it would on me."

"Guess then that it's a lucky thing you're both related to half the police department and know they have your back," Esteban commented.

Sean looked toward his daughter. "Straighten him out, Kari. I've got a crime scene to process." With that, he walked into the town house.

Kari turned her attention to her partner, wondering if he was being sarcastic, reflective, or—? It was still early in the game, but she sincerely wished she was able to read Fernandez better.

But her father was right. In case he was being cynical, he needed to be set straight.

"They'd have our back even if we weren't related. Just like they have yours." She saw the skeptical look in his eyes. "I think you've been on your own too long, Fernandez. I think your superiors pulled you out just in time."

"I don't," he retorted darkly.

She stared at him. Was he being serious, or just playing the macho card? "You do realize that it was just a matter of time—hours—before you were killed if they hadn't," she told him, refusing to believe that he actually meant what he'd just said.

"Maybe," Esteban qualified in a way that indicated he was far from convinced that would have been his fate.

"The cartel *made* you," she stressed. "That means they knew you were a cop," she said needlessly. "How can you possibly think that their plans for you didn't involve a cold slab and being plowed six feet under in some unmarked grave?" she demanded.

Did he think he was some kind of superhero who could defy bullets and death?

He was not about to have that argument here, especially not with her. "Let's change the subject," he ground out, abruptly ending the conversation.

Kari didn't want to change the subject. She wanted to hammer away at this numbskull with the beautiful eyes until she got him to see reason. But having been raised with four brothers had taught her how futile it was to argue with a man who had stubbornly made up his mind—even if he was terminally wrong.

"Okay," she allowed with forced cheerfulness, then couldn't resist adding, "for now."

It earned her another formidable look, which she pretended not to see.

Back to the case, she thought. That was the important thing.

"Let's see if we can find out if the victim's granddaughter is up to talking yet. Maybe she can give us a list of Mae's friends." She sighed, knowing that route usually led nowhere—but she had to try. "Who knows? Maybe we'll get lucky and someone knows something they don't know they know."

Esteban shot her a sideways glance that told her what he thought of that idea, but he fell in step with her anyway.

They were just about to get back into the car in order to drive to the hospital where the distraught young woman had been taken when one of the crime scene investigators came hurrying out of the town house, calling to them to get their attention.

Tall and thin to the point of being almost gaunt, and with a mop of unruly dirty-blond hair that made him resemble a giant Q-tip, Silas Baker waved his hand over his head to make his presence known in case they couldn't hear him.

They could.

"Detectives!"

They both turned from the car and looked in the investigator's direction. The young man—Kari judged that he had to be younger than she was, which made him pretty young in her book—beckoned them forward.

"The boss found something he thought you might

be interested in," Silas volunteered with barely contained excitement.

His enthusiasm told her that he was new on the job. Kari quickened her pace, getting to the doorway a beat before her partner did.

Assuming that whatever it was her father had discovered and wanted them to see was at the heart of the crime scene, she headed back to the kitchen once she reentered the town house.

"Find something?" she asked her father, crossing to his side.

He'd just finished a very cursory examination of the body, taking care to be gentle and respectful of the dead. "Thought you might be interested in this. I found it clutched in the victim's hand." He addressed his words to both of them as he held out a see-through plastic envelope, the kind that was used to bag and tag evidence for cataloging.

Since she was closest to her father, Kari took the evidence bag and looked at it. At first glance, the bag appeared to contain a tiny charm, like the kind that could be found on an old-fashioned charm bracelet.

The sunlight coming in through the window over the sink hit the charm dead-on, making it glimmer like a ray of trapped sunshine.

"Okay," she said gamely, not quite sure what she was supposed to see when she looked at it—and then she focused on the charm for the first time. Her heart thudded when she realized what it was supposed to be. "Oh, God, it's a tiny scales of justice," she breathed.

"So much for the copycat idea," Esteban muttered, striking the theory off the board. "Looks like our killer is going on with his game."

"Killing people isn't a game," Kari snapped, momentarily losing her temper because she felt so powerless to stop the murderer before he struck again. That he would murder once more was a near certainty at this point.

"It might be to him," Esteban countered, his voice devoid of any emotion.

She looked at him sharply. Didn't he *feel* anything? she wondered angrily.

"He's right," Sean told her, his voice low and steady, exhibiting how cool he always was, even under pressure. "This could be just a sick game to the killer, and until we know otherwise, that might be useful to keep in mind."

She knew what the word "game" implied. "That would make the killer a cold-blooded sociopath."

His tone didn't change, but the expression on her father's face was grim. "Exactly."

Taking out her phone, Kari took a picture of the encased charm, then handed the evidence bag back to her father. The item had to be cataloged as evidence, but she wanted to show the photo to the victim's granddaughter. She needed to find out whether the charm belonged to the victim...or if the killer had planted it in her hand rather than draw the symbol on her the way he had on William Reynolds.

"Thanks," she said to her father, checking to see if the photograph had turned out clear. Satisfied, she put her cell phone away.

"No need for thanks. We're on the same team, remember?" her father pointed out as he handed off the tagged charm to Silas, the tall, gangly investigator who had called them back. The latter locked away the evidence in his own meticulously organized black case.

"I need a reminder every now and then," Kari told her father, only half kidding.

Rather than answer with a quip, her father replied, "I know," just before he got back to work.

Esteban was silent as they walked back to the car and remained that way for the first couple of miles as they drove to the nearest hospital, where the victim's granddaughter would have been taken.

Finally, ten minutes into the trip, he asked, "What did you mean by 'still'?" and caught Kari completely off guard.

Because they hadn't exchanged a single word since they'd left the crime scene, Kari had no idea what he was referring to. Confused, she glanced in his direction before looking back at the road.

"What are you talking about?" she demanded.

After clearing his throat a couple of times, Esteban tried again. "You said you were surprised to find out that I still had some compassion in me. The word 'still' would mean that you thought you already knew me."

"I did." She could see that wasn't the answer he wanted. "Want to go somewhere and pick up a late lunch?" she asked.

Until she'd mentioned it, he hadn't realized that as of yet, they hadn't stopped to eat and it was getting closer to dinnertime than to lunch. "What about Anne Daniels?" he asked, referring to the victim's traumatized granddaughter.

"Have you been to a hospital lately?" she asked him. "I'm sure she'll still be there in an hour when we get there."

With a shrug, Esteban said, "Okay, why not?" and assumed that the subject of his so-called recognition was being tabled. Which was just as well, he decided. It would only complicate things.

Kari asked softly, "You don't remember me, do you?"

For now, Esteban intended to play it very close to the vest. "Should I?"

She answered his question with a question of her own. "What high school did you go to?"

Accustomed to covering up every detail of his life and keeping it hidden at all costs, his immediate reaction was to go on the defensive. "What difference does that make?" he contested.

"Plenty," she told him with feeling. "I went to Aurora High. The quarterback there my first two years was this Adonis with an incredible throwing arm. To watch him play football was like watching poetry in motion."

She watched him carefully, waiting to see if there was any kind of reaction to her words. He remained as stoic as a statue. "He had midnight-black hair that was a little on the long side, and I knew of several girls who would have killed just to run their fingers through it…or simply have him smile in their direction."

"Does that include you?" The question came out of the blue and succeeded in catching her off guard for a second time.

She felt a wave of heat pass over her. Since it was a mild spring day, the weather was not a factor in the abrupt change in temperature. "I had a crush on him," she admitted, knowing she had to answer him honestly. "But I could never get myself to be part of a crowd. Because I was already one of seven at home, I was always trying too hard to be noticed as an individual." She kept on studying his facial features, waiting for a glimmer, for some sort of an indication that she was right. "His name was Steve Fernandez."

He shrugged indifferently. "Fernandez is a common last name."

"So you're saying that wasn't you," she challenged.

He stared straight ahead. The teenager he had been seemed like someone from another lifetime. His world had undergone drastic changes since then. And he had

had to struggle every day to keep on putting one foot in front of the other.

And maybe the answer to healing was shedding his identity altogether. "I'm saying that wasn't me."

She saw the minuscule way his jaw tightened, saw the lone nerve along his cheek move spasmodically. *That* was her answer, not the words he said.

"It *was* you," she said quietly.

He shot her a look. "If that's an indication of your detective instincts, I'd say as a team, we're in big trouble and I'm within my rights to ask for another partner."

"Think another partner would put up with you any better than I would?" she wanted to know, her tone deceptively mild.

Esteban blew out a breath.

Rather than answer her question or even acknowledge it, he quoted an old adage he knew: "I guess better the devil you know than the devil you don't know."

Kari laughed shortly, amused despite herself. "First time I've been referred to as the devil. You'd be a big hit with my brothers, you know." Pausing for a moment, she looked at him just before she started up the car. "So we're good?"

"We're good, Hyphen," he said, slanting a glance in her direction.

She still wasn't warming up to the nickname, but she supposed that things could be a lot worse. "Okay, slight change in plans," she announced. "Let's go see how the victim's granddaughter is doing first, *then* pick up some takeout and bring it to the station. This way we can eat and go over what we've learned so far." She paused for a second, then added, "Steve."

He looked at her sharply then. She could see that he wanted to say something in response, maybe even chastise her for addressing him by a name he'd clearly disavowed. But she also knew that her new partner couldn't have survived undercover for the length of time that he had by allowing his temper to get the better of him.

What he did say to her when he finally spoke was "I'm not your quarterback."

She smiled at that, thinking how, back in the day, the very idea that he was hers would have had her walking at least three inches off the ground.

"I never said the quarterback was mine," Kari pointed out.

Esteban said nothing. She had a feeling that was because he really didn't know what to say.

Score one for the home team, Kari thought.

His beautiful, feisty partner had managed to hit far too close to home and that made him uncomfortable. As far as he was concerned, the life he'd had before he'd gone undercover was dead and gone and bringing it up now after all this time just succeeded in exhuming all the hurt, all the pain that he'd buried almost four years ago.

All the hurt and pain that *had* to remain buried in

order for him to function at least moderately well as a cop.

He gave serious consideration to asking for a new partner, but he needed a reason and citing something as inane as irreconcilable differences was beyond ridiculous. And he couldn't very well tell the Chief of D's that his niece recognized him from their school days, blowing the last of his carefully constructed cover, because that sounded worse than lame.

So, for now, he knew he had no other choice but to ride it out, and stay confident that keeping to himself would eventually push her to ask for a new partner. He just hoped that the confounding feeling bedeviling him—the one he was doing his best to ignore—wouldn't trip him up and wreak havoc on the life he'd worked so hard to strip bare.

Yet even as he tried not to think about it—about her—he found that it was far easier said than done.

Chapter 9

"That's not hers."

Tears flowing freely, the woman propped up in the hospital bed pushed away the photograph that Kari and Esteban were showing her.

Kari held the photo of the charm in front of Anne Daniels again, not entirely convinced that the woman was thinking clearly.

"You're sure?" she pressed. "Look at the picture carefully."

"I don't have to. My grandmother didn't like jewelry." The young woman angrily pushed the photograph away again. "She didn't own any. She thought it was a waste of money that could be spent in better

ways, like supporting children's charities." Her voice
shook as she spoke. "She was always doing things
like that...volunteering her time to help mentor kids
from underprivileged neighborhoods, starting up food
drives and collecting toys around the holidays. People
are really going to miss her." Anne pressed her lips
together to keep a sob back as fresh tears fell.

When she was in control again, the bereaved
woman nodded at the photograph and asked, "Where
did you find that?"

"The charm was clutched in your grandmother's
hand," Esteban explained, stepping up beside Kari to
make his presence known

Confusion crept across Anne's features as she
looked from one detective to the other. "That doesn't
make any sense." And then a possible explanation
seemed to dawn on her. "Maybe the killer was wearing it and she managed to snatch it from him while
she was struggling. Oh, God." She covered her mouth
as she tried to stifle a fresh wave of sobs.

"Maybe," Kari allowed. That could be one theory,
she supposed. As good as any other so far.

A hopeful look entered the woman's brown eyes.
It was obvious she wanted nothing more than to find
her grandmother's killer. "Then that makes the charm
a clue, right?"

"We can hope," Kari told the other woman as gently
as she could.

Taking the bull by the horns, Esteban had some

questions of his own to ask the victim's granddaughter. "Do you know if anyone ever threatened your grandmother? Vowed to get even with her for some slight they thought she had committed against them?"

Anne vehemently shook her head to each question, and then insisted, "No, no. My grandmother went out of her way to be nice to everyone. Everyone loved her," she repeated. Unable to stop the tears that kept coming, she wiped them away with the edge of her sheet.

"Not everyone," Esteban pointed out bluntly.

That brought on even more tears of anguish.

Appalled by his insensitivity, Kari glared at Esteban. His expression remained stoic. She knew it was his way of creating a barrier between himself and the rest of the world, but he was merely making a bad situation worse. And since they clearly weren't getting anywhere with the victim's granddaughter, Kari decided they needed to back off and let her grieve in peace.

"If you think of anything else—or just need to talk—you can reach me at this number anytime," Kari said, indicating the bottom number on the card that she'd just placed on the bed beside Anne Daniels.

The woman pressed her lips together, obviously too choked up to talk. Picking up the card, she nodded silently, looking as if her whole world had shattered.

"You keep handing those cards out like that, you're going to wind up holding shrink sessions in the back of your car," Esteban commented as they walked through the hospital lobby, headed for the exit and the parking lots beyond the eight-story building.

Kari didn't see it that way. "People need to feel that they're not alone."

Was she really that naive? he wondered. Or just some cockeyed optimist who didn't know which end was up? Either way, she needed to be set straight.

"People *are* alone," he told her firmly.

"Maybe so," she conceded, because she didn't want to get sucked into a philosophical argument neither side intended to lose. Instead, she emphasized, "But they don't have to feel that way."

Esteban laughed shortly. "So you're going to kiss their hurts, put Band-Aids on them and make them all better?"

He was baiting her, she thought, which was why she managed to remain unfazed. "If it helps, I can be there to listen."

"And if you're so busy 'listening,' when are you going to do your job? Or don't you intend to ever sleep?" he asked.

"I've learned how to catnap," she countered, keeping her own expression unreadable.

Kari paused for a moment as they got into the car. She knew she was going to be treading on dangerous ground, but she was never going to find any answers by keeping quiet.

"What you said before," she began. "About people being alone…is that how you really feel?"

He didn't appreciate her probing him. "I wouldn't have said it if I didn't," he bit off.

"*Do* you feel alone?" she pressed.

How many different ways did she want him to say it? He was beginning to think that saying anything at all had been a huge mistake.

"Back off, Hyphen," he warned, his eyes narrowing. "I don't need a shrink."

Not every psychiatrist turned out to be helpful, and she knew without being told that her partner was not the sort who would ever seek help to begin with. "No, but maybe you need a friend."

"What I *need*," he emphasized, "is a partner—if I have to have one—who doesn't talk so much."

She smiled. Slowly but surely, she was beginning to understand him—at least a little. It allowed her to say, "Well, there I'm afraid that you're out of luck."

Esteban slanted a long look in her direction, then faced forward, gazing out the windshield without really seeing anything.

"Don't count on it," he told her.

She took a deep breath, summoned her courage and forced herself to ask, "What happened between high school and here?"

"Life," was all he said. He made the single word sound ominous and volatile. He also didn't trust himself to say more.

Turning the key, she started up the car and backed out of the space. "What—?"

"Drop it, Hyphen," he ordered. His voice left no room for any give-and-take. That part of the game was over.

She'd pushed him as far as he'd go today, Kari realized. There was always tomorrow, but in order to get to tomorrow, she had to remain his partner today.

She backed off.

"You in the mood for Mexican or Chinese?" Kari asked cheerfully, thinking of the two best take-out places between the hospital and the police station.

He'd never been ruled by his taste buds and he shrugged now in answer to her question. "Doesn't matter," he told her.

"You don't have a preference?" Kari asked, clearly surprised.

When he was hungry, he ate what was in front of him. "Not worth the time picking one over the other," he said, then added, "You pick."

"Okay," she answered after a beat. "I will."

Esteban stared at the chopsticks his partner held out to him. Served him right for abdicating control. "What makes you think I want to spear my food like some backward hunter?"

"Pretty limited hunting grounds," she pointed out. "Besides, I thought maybe you knew how to use them." Everyone she knew was fairly proficient with chopsticks, so she'd just assumed he was, too.

She should have known better, she upbraided herself.

"I suppose you do." The way he said it was almost an accusation—if not an indictment.

She refused to let him make her feel guilty because she knew how to do something he didn't. "It's really not that hard once you pick it up."

"Well, I didn't pick it up—and I don't intend to," he added stubbornly. If he had a pet peeve—and he absolutely *hated* that term—it was people who tried to change him to suit their needs.

As Kari nodded, she opened up a side drawer and took out a wrapped, white plastic utensil. "How do you feel about a plastic fork?"

"I don't have feelings about utensils," he informed her crisply, nonetheless taking the white plastic fork she offered.

Kari shook her head. It was hard to reconcile this rough-spoken man with the laughing, jovial senior she remembered. "Boy, if Marnie Wilson could only see you now."

Esteban looked up from his lunch, a scowl furrowing his brow. "Who's Marnie Wilson?"

She hadn't really expected him to remember the name. "She was one of the adoring females who had a mad crush on you in high school. She was sure that you walked on water on a regular basis."

He gave her a disgruntled look. "I told you, I'm not this guy you're talking about."

Yes, he was. She would have been willing to bet her soul on that.

But because she didn't feel like getting embroiled in yet another argument with him today, she merely nodded. "Whatever you say, Fernandez."

"Finally," he declared. "First agreeable thing I've heard you say all day."

"Then you haven't been listening," she countered with a grin that was far too wide.

It was time to get back to work. Nibbling on the spring roll in her hand, she walked over to the bulletin board she had so painstakingly put together after they came back to the precinct.

"What is it that these two victims have in common that got under the killer's skin?" she asked, the question directed more to herself than to her devilishly handsome partner.

"Okay." It was obvious he'd been giving the matter a lot of thought, as well. "They're both retired. By other people's accounts, they both do volunteer work of some sort, although it sounds like she apparently did more than he did." Esteban looked over at Kari, winding up his summary. "And they're both dead."

Kari sighed. "Besides that." She chewed on her lower lip for a moment, thinking, completely oblivious to the fact that she looked damn sensual doing it.

But Esteban wasn't oblivious to it, despite the fact that he wanted to be.

She ran down the list of possibilities. "Maybe they

both go to the same church, the same club, the same supermarket."

The last place sounded almost too ludicrous for consideration. "And what? A clerk decided to kill them for squeezing the produce too hard?" Esteban cracked.

Kari spared him a glare as she returned to her desk, frustrated. Picking up the carton of fried rice, she dove in. She was eating without tasting her food or being fully aware that she actually *was* eating.

It was all part of her thinking process.

"No, but there has to be some common denominator that we're not seeing. Slashing someone's throat is a very particular way of killing them. Seems almost intimate. It *has* to mean something."

Esteban found himself agreeing. "Whoever it is has assumed the role of judge, jury and executioner," he speculated. When she raised a puzzled eyebrow, silently asking for an explanation, he obliged. "That's why the killer drew the scales of justice on the first victim and left that charm in the second victim's hand."

"Why a charm?" she wanted to know. "He'd have to buy it and risk someone remembering him doing it."

"Not if he got it online," Esteban said. "There're countless sites selling things like this."

"Why go through the trouble of getting the charm in the first place?" she pressed, curious to see what he would come up with.

"So that he gets his point across," Esteban insisted.

"That first drawing on Reynolds wasn't all that clear and the blood almost obliterated it. It could have easily been missed. He wants us to know he's taking the law into his own hands and is dispensing justice because the law failed him somehow."

She looked at him, nodding. He could actually be on to something there.

"Hey, you're pretty good at this when you put your mind to it," she complimented. "I'm impressed."

He looked at her, less than thrilled. "I'm not trying to impress you, I'm trying to get this psycho off the street."

Well, at least they were in agreement on that point, she thought. "Nevertheless, I'm impressed anyway," she told him. "Consider it icing on the cake."

The laugh was less than warm. Warmth came, though, when she looked into his eyes. "Icing rots your teeth," he told her.

Kari shook her head. Roguishly good-looking or not, how was she supposed to survive this partnership? "God, but you are a downer."

He saw the look in her eyes, saw another question all but bubbling on her lips. She was going to ask him again what had made him this way. The memory was far too painful to unearth.

"Leave it alone, Hyphen," he warned in a low voice, "or you'll be looking for a new partner."

She raised her hands as if in surrender and glibly said, "Okay, this is me, leaving it alone."

He snorted, knowing that this wasn't the last of it. People like Kari got things in their head and kept after it no matter what. Approaching it at all different directions, all different angles, until the item finally cracked open and was theirs.

But at least he'd gotten her to drop the subject for now and that was all he was asking for. Just a few short hours of respite.

Kari debated what her next step should be. Not with the investigation—she knew what to do there—but to get to the bottom of what exactly had transformed the charismatic high school quarterback she remembered into the sullen, brooding man she'd been partnered up with.

She knew she could always go back to Brenda. But she'd already imposed on her enough. Granted that the woman was the Chief of Detectives' daughter-in-law, which meant that she wasn't going to get into any trouble on the force unless she killed someone. But she didn't want to put Brenda on the spot by asking her to delve into closed files that were deemed to be secret and redacted.

Besides, she needed to save the savvy computer tech for bigger things. No, this time around she was going to have to find another venue to obtain her information.

Still chewing on the problem of Fernandez's drastic transformation, she decided to approach the man who in her opinion had all the answers. If there was an answer to dispense, the call, one way or another, was ultimately his.

Squaring her shoulders and summoning her courage, Kari went to see the Chief of Detectives.

Brian Cavanaugh was about to finally call it a day. His wife was waiting for him at their favorite restaurant. It was his way of paying her back for putting up with all the long hours that he was on the job and away from home. But then, Lila understood.

He'd met Lila on the force years ago. Eventually, she became his partner and after almost dying in his arms when she was shot by an enraged gunman, Lila was assigned to a desk job. But even there she knew all about the demands that were made on a law enforcement officer, especially a high-ranking one.

In all the years they'd been together, he'd never once heard her complain. But that didn't mean that there weren't times when she was rightfully resentful of having to share him with an entire department of men and women—and usually getting the short end of the stick.

So when he saw his brother's daughter, Kari, standing in the doorway of his office, Brian was surprised as well as somewhat impatient.

With effort he banked down the latter for the moment and said, "I'm on my way out, Kari. Is there something I can do for you?"

Talk about awful timing, she thought with dread.

"I can come back," she volunteered.

"Is this something that I can handle quickly?" he wanted to know. He'd never liked putting things off if he could help it. He'd learned the hard way that regrets were often tied to procrastination.

"That depends on your answer," she told him honestly, rather than giving a blanket yes so that he would feel obligated to help her, only to discover that the matter needed more time than he could accommodate.

"On my answer to what?" Brian asked as he sat down behind his desk again. He was prepared to allow her fifteen minutes, the same he would allow any other police officer who came to him. His goal ever since he'd taken on this position was to treat everyone fairly.

"What's Detective Fernandez's story?"

He looked at her for a long moment, trying to ascertain exactly what she meant by that. "Which part?"

She stated it as succinctly as she could. "The part that changed him from a popular high school jock who got along with everyone to the scowling, closemouthed man riding around in my car."

Something Kari had just said caught his attention. "You knew Fernandez before you were introduced the other day?"

Before Esteban had first partnered up with her, she would have said yes immediately. Now she felt she had to qualify her answer just a little.

"I believe I did, yes. But when I knew him, he

wasn't anything like this, so it's hard for me to be sure. And, with the investigation in full swing, I don't have the luxury of time to find out if it *is* the same man." She threw up her hands in exasperation. "It *looks* like him and the name's the same, but there's a world of difference between the two. And if it is the same man, I just want to know what happened to change him so drastically."

Brian nodded, taking in not only her words, but the expression on her face as she said them. "And wondering about this is interfering with your work?"

Was he telling her that it wasn't any of her business and had no place on the job? She pushed ahead anyway. "Let's just say I'm having trouble focusing a hundred and ten percent on the case."

"Why don't you just ask Fernandez?" he asked. It seemed like the simplest way to go, if somewhat awkward, a situation he was all too familiar with.

"I did," she insisted. "He doesn't want to talk about it."

"Then maybe you should respect his wishes."

There was more to it than that, and she wanted her uncle to understand that this wasn't just idle curiosity on her part. "It's hard to tread lightly when I don't really know what subject I'm avoiding."

"Fair enough," Brian conceded. He didn't have to look into the matter and get back to her later. He already knew the man's history. He made it a point to know the backstory for *all* his law enforcement officers when he dealt with them. "When he was away at college, his younger brother, Julio, died of a drug overdose. His stepfather was so grief-stricken, he hunted the drug dealer down and shot him. The dealer's boss retaliated by killing Fernandez's mother. His stepfather was sent to prison.

"Esteban felt entirely helpless. The only way he could cope with what had happened was to go deep underground to bring the cartel down. But a week ago, as you know, his cover was blown so we had to pull him out. That didn't sit too well with him."

"That part I knew. The rest of it—" She blew out a long breath, shaking her head. "Wow. That seems like too much for one person to handle."

"My thoughts exactly. I'm surprised that he didn't just come apart at the seams." He looked at her with a very intuitive expression on his face. "If anyone can help him come around, you can."

She doubted it, despite the fact that the compliment felt good. "I think you have entirely too much faith in me, sir."

"I don't," Brian countered. "Now, if you'll excuse me, I have to meet a beautiful woman for dinner before she gets tired of waiting for me and goes home."

Kari quickly vacated her seat. "Thanks for taking the time to talk to me, Chief," she said, walking out with him.

"Anytime, Kari. Anytime."

She felt he meant it. Backup, she thought, was a wonderful thing.

"What's going on with you, Pop?" Andrew Cavanaugh asked his father as he came out to the patio carrying two bottles of chilled beer. He handed one to his father, then took a seat next to him. The teak rocker creaked a little as he sank down. Andrew made a mental note to oil the hinges with silicone later.

Shamus cocked a puzzled brow as he regarded his oldest son. Taking a long swig from the bottle first, he asked, "What d'you mean 'what's going on?'"

The question was just a little too innocent, his father's attitude just a wee bit too defensive. He was right, Andrew thought. Something *was* up.

"You look a little off your game, Dad," he told him, then took a guess at the cause. "The security business not exactly living up to your expectations? Maybe a little too tame for you?"

Shamus laughed as he studied the condensation on the side of the bottle. "I lived in a retirement community in Boca Raton for eight years, Andy. *Anything's* more exciting than that."

They'd take it slow, Andrew determined. His father never liked saying anything straight out. "Actually, I'm surprised you waited that long to strike out of that place." Although, he had to admit that by the end of the seventh year, it looked as if his father had turned over a new leaf and decided that the quiet life was more to his liking.

"'Strike out?' Hell, boy, I *ran* away from there." He grinned, pleased with himself and the action he'd taken in that respect. "Far as I know, those people who ran the place are still looking for me."

If that was the case, then he would have already received a call from the woman who oversaw the community, asking if he'd seen his father. He had a feeling that the people in charge had breathed a sigh of relief when Shamus had left.

"You might want to go back there," Andrew suggested, "clear things up, move out your things."

"Anything of value I had I took with me. Far as I'm concerned, they can have the rest. I don't intend to set foot in that place again." For a moment, he paused, watching as the sun began to dip in the sky, preparing to set. Sunrises and sunsets always filled him with wonder. At his age, he was grateful to see each one. "Besides, I've got more important things on my mind."

Now they were getting to it, Andrew thought. "Like what?"

Shamus took another pull from his bottle. "Andy, you ever think about expanding this security firm that you've set up?"

Well, he hadn't seen this coming. "I already have. As the company got more clients, I hired on more guards, more software techs to monitor the security systems."

"No, not that kind of expanding," Shamus said with a touch of impatience as he shook his shaggy head.

His father had momentarily lost him. "What other kind is there?"

Warming to his topic, Shamus leaned forward, closer to his son. "Adding another wing to the business," he said, mystified that Andrew couldn't see that. "Like private investigations."

"Are you talking about having private detectives, Pop?" Andrew asked.

Shamus's face lit up. "Glad to see we're on the same page," he declared heartily.

Andrew held his hand up, as if to slow his father down for a bit. "I'm not on a page, Pop, I'm just looking at the title on top." He'd begun the company with a certain focus in mind, providing decent, affordable security for the average family, and, as far as he was concerned, he was accomplishing that. "Why would I want to have private detectives?"

His father looked at him as if the answer was self-evident. "Well, most of the guys who work for you are retired cops. The way I see it, having a private detective section available to your clients would just be a natural progression of things."

A hint of amusement played across Andrew's face. "Oh, you do, do you?"

"Yes, I do," Shamus affirmed with feeling.

Andrew felt as if he was back on the force, trying

to draw reliable information out of a witness. "And just what kind of 'things' do you see us investigating?"

Shamus shrugged his wide shoulders, then took another long pull from his bottle.

He was stalling, Andrew thought. Why? For dramatic effect? Or because this was hard for him to talk about?

"Oh, I dunno," Shamus finally said loftily. "Maybe specialize in locating lost family members, that kind of thing."

It was time to get to the heart of the matter. His father, now that he thought about it, had the ability to dance around a topic all night. "What's this really about, Pop?"

"Can't a father look out for his son's interest?" Shamus asked, growing defensive again.

"Sure he can," Andrew responded soothingly. "And I appreciate it, I do." He eyed his father as he continued. "He can also level with his son, which would be even *more* appreciated."

Shamus laughed self-consciously. Andrew saw right through his roundabout approach. "Once a cop, always a cop, huh?"

"Something like that," Andrew conceded. "Now give, Pop. What's on your mind? *Why* do you need a private investigator? Investigating what?"

Shamus grew quiet, thoughtfully regarding the near empty bottle of beer. He tilted it to and fro, watching the remaining liquid inside move from one side of the bottle to the other. Finally, he asked, "You remember my telling you about your grandfather and grandmother?"

"You told me Grandpa was a homicide detective, that he liked to drink a little more than he should and that was why he and his wife split up." People took a dim view of divorce back then, usually condemning the woman because it meant that she didn't try hard enough to keep her marriage together. He knew his father hadn't had an easy time of it, coming from a broken home. He'd turned out incredibly well-adjusted and kind, given what he'd had to endure.

There was no humor to the smile that was now on his lips. "Your grandfather used to like to drink a lot more than he should," Shamus corrected. "My mother put up with it as long as she could, and then she just took off," he said, his voice sounding as hollow as he'd felt at the time of his abandonment.

It was time to call him out, and then end this, Andrew decided. "Okay. Where's this going, Pop?"

Each word he uttered left a bitter taste on his tongue. "Well, when she took off, my mother took my younger brother with her."

Very few things surprised Andrew. At this point in his life, he'd seen and heard it all, far more than the average citizen. But this caught him completely off guard.

"You had a younger brother?" Andrew asked,

stunned by the words his father had just uttered. "Why didn't you ever tell me?"

At first it seemed as if his father hadn't even heard his question. "At the time I was pretty hurt that she took Jonny and left me. I kept waiting, night after night, for her to come back, to say she'd made a mistake and meant to take me with her instead—or at least too. After a year, I decided she wasn't coming back, that she'd left me with Dad on purpose because she didn't want to have anything to do with either one of us." He looked at Andrew, shame and sadness mingling in his eyes. "I didn't tell you or your brothers about it because I was ashamed that your grandmother didn't think I was worth taking with her."

Andrew didn't see it that way and it hurt to see how wounded his father was by this even after all these years. "Could have been a lot of reasons why she picked him over you," he offered. "From what you said, your brother was younger. Maybe he was sickly."

The shaggy head moved from side to side. "Nope."

Andrew wasn't about to give up. "Still could have been a logical reason why she chose him and left you. Maybe she thought you were strong enough to look after your dad because he needed someone to keep him from drinking himself to death."

Shamus blew out a breath as he shook his head. "I doubt if she was being that thoughtful, but thanks for trying."

"Does this have anything to do with you wanting

to expand the security company?" Andrew asked, trying to tie the whole thing together and get his father talking about the present rather than just exclusively the past.

"Absolutely," Shamus said with feeling. "I'm in my seventies, Andy. I don't know just how much time I've got left—"

"About thirty years," Andrew countered without even a hint of a smile. "If they don't catch a bullet," he continued, thinking of his late brother, Mike, who had died in the line of duty, "Cavanaughs are generally very long-lived."

The key word here being "generally," Shamus thought. "Yeah, well, until I find that carved in stone by the Big Guy," he nodded toward the sky, "I'm going to move forward as if there're no guarantees on that."

For now, he tabled the discussion on how much time he had left. That wasn't the important part. "Anyway, I want to have Jonny tracked down, see what happened to him, if he's still alive. If he ever got married and had any kids. It's been bothering me lately, not knowing," Shamus confessed.

He could well understand that—and sympathize with it. "I don't have to expand the company for that," Andrew told his father.

"No, but it's not a bad idea," Shamus insisted, then pointed out, "That way, we'd have all these resources available to us twenty-four/seven. And the investigator would be on your clock, not someone else's," he pointed out. "People tend to do better for their own than for some stranger who hires them."

"Worth thinking about," Andrew agreed, then suggested, "Until then, though, why don't you give me all the information you do have on this long lost brother of yours? That way, I can start looking into it for you." He saw the skeptical look slipped over his father's face. "Don't give me that look, Pop. I tracked down Rose, remember? Everyone told me to give up, that she was dead and I was just torturing myself by not accepting it. But I refused to listen because we never found a body when Rose's car went over the embankment.

"And," he added triumphantly, "everyone else was wrong and I was right."

"Right about what, dear?" Rose asked as she came out to the patio to join her husband and father-in-law. They'd been out here for a while now and dusk had settled in like a warm throw on a chilly autumn evening. It was time to find out what was going on.

"Right about saying that you're the best thing that ever happened to me," Andrew volunteered, holding the bottle of beer aloft as he pulled her onto his lap with his other hand.

She knew when she was being kept in the dark. She also knew that it was never anything major, so for now, she played along.

"Can't argue with that," she said, giving her husband a quick kiss. And then she looked from her father-in-law to her husband. "But what are you two *really* talking about?"

"Expanding the company," Andrew answered. For now, the fact that he might have an uncle floating out there would remain between his father and him. He had a feeling that his father wasn't quite ready to share his secret with the rest of the family just yet.

Rose thought for a moment, then nodded. "Sounds like a good idea," she agreed.

Shamus beamed. Leaning forward again, he gave his daughter-in-law's hand a quick squeeze. "Always said I liked this girl."

Rose laughed. "And I really like being called that," she told her father-in-law.

Andrew watched the two interact, amused. But he never took even one moment he had with Rose for granted.

Even so, the wheels in his head were furiously turning as he considered the investigation he was about to undertake.

A long lost uncle, who would have ever thought it?

Chapter 10

Years of working on his own had predisposed Esteban to working best alone.

Which was why he thought he'd get an early start this morning and come in while the office was still empty. But the moment he walked into the squad room, he saw that he'd thought wrong.

Because it was more than an hour before the morning shift came on, the rest of the area was still empty. However, the desk butted up directly against his was not. Kari was there, although it was anyone's guess whether she was conscious or not. She'd obviously put her head down to grab a few winks.

Apparently the winks were still going on. Her head was resting on her arms, which she'd drawn close together and crossed in order to afford herself a tiny bit of comfort.

Not that they would give her all that much, he judged. From what he'd seen of them, her arms were rather toned. It was obvious that she liked to keep herself fit. He could relate to that.

He could almost, he thought, relate to her, as well.

Though he wouldn't admit it to her, she was right about remembering him from high school. All sorts of memories came flooding back to him. They *had* gone to school together, although he'd been a year ahead of her.

Even so, they'd shared a couple of academic classes. He might have been a jock back then, but he was determined to use his athletic abilities to propel him up the road to getting a higher education. Securing a football scholarship meant he could spend more time studying, less time working to pay for that education. He'd set his sights on lofty goals.

And she was a junior with looks and brains—and if he recalled correctly, she'd been far more interested in using those brains, rather than her feminine wiles, to get ahead. He found that admirable.

And, at the time, rare.

He also remembered another very pertinent thing about her. She was *not* part of the circle of girls he had found perpetually clustered around him. She was always off somewhere in the background. He'd catch her looking his way once in a while. Looking, but not joining.

He remembered wondering if she was shy.

He also vaguely remembered being intrigued by her. But there were so many more willing and available girls back then that he didn't have time to find out what her story was.

Even though he'd wanted to.

And then he'd graduated and gone off to college.

But those brilliant blue eyes of hers, and that certain tilt of her head when she smiled—that he remembered. That stayed with him.

Now that all seemed like it had happened a hundred years ago, he thought, putting the tall container of coffee he'd bought at the coffee shop down on his desk. The person he'd been, that jock with the world at his feet—that was someone else from another lifetime.

The life he now had had begun when he'd been called out of his class at the academy and taken aside by the chief of police. The man—ironically the brother of the current Chief of D's—had told him as gently as he could about his mother and brother's deaths and what his stepfather had done to avenge Julio.

It had all taken place within a twenty-four-hour period.

Only twenty-four hours. And just like that, the light had gone out of his life.

Out of his world.

Avenging his family by taking down all the members of the cartel that he could seemed like the only reason for him to go on drawing breath. So he'd done just that. And he'd done it well.

And then, even that had been taken away from him.

The Chief was right. He'd had to flee or die. As if the latter mattered.

Every morning, he got up, wondering why. And yet, he did…and he found himself putting one foot in front of the other. And, these past few days, somehow arriving here. To work with a vibrant woman he pretended not to recognize.

Sometimes he wondered if all sense had left his world, as well.…

Drawn back to the present, he couldn't help but note that Kari was still out like a light. She must have put in one long night.

Rounding his desk, he came around to her side and lightly tapped his partner on the shoulder. When that didn't seem to rouse her, he did it again, a little harder this time.

He was about to do it a third time—it was either that or yell in her ear—when Kari abruptly jerked her head up from her desk, as if suddenly aware of not being alone anymore.

She looked up at him and blinked, trying to focus eyes that were still somewhat blurry from lack of a decent night's sleep. She was acutely conscious of his almost overpowering aura. That, and his intense blue eyes. With effort, she struggled to pull herself together.

"You spend the night here?" Esteban asked gruffly.

It was a rhetorical question. She was wearing the same thing she'd had on yesterday, so unless she was particularly attached to the light blue pencil skirt and jacket, she hadn't gone home to sleep or even to get a change of clothes.

God, but her neck hurt, Kari thought as a razor-sharp pain speared through her. She rubbed her hand across the area, trying to get back a little feeling into it. She wasn't having much luck. Kari stifled a gasp when she felt his hands on her neck, kneading and creating more tense muscles than he was eliminating. She pulled away.

"I'm okay," she said a bit too quickly. The last thing she needed was having him touch her like that. "I guess I must have fallen asleep," she muttered. She certainly hadn't intended to do that when she'd sat down at her desk last night. She had only wanted to review a few things, but as usual, time had gotten away from her.

"Is that for me, or did you just decide to redecorate yourself?" he asked, allowing a glimmer of amusement to show through.

When she looked at him, obviously confused by his question, Esteban leaned over and plucked off the Post-it note that had somehow gotten itself attached to her forehead. He held it up for her to see.

There was nothing written on it.

"Using invisible ink again?" he drawled.

"Keep it," she muttered. She didn't recall writing a note to anyone. "Consider it a gift."

He glanced down at the steaming-hot coffee on his desk. The lid was still on, but tiny whiffs of steam were escaping from the sides.

"Here." He picked up the container and placed it on her desk. "I think you need this more than I do."

Removing the lid, she proceeded to take the container into both her hands as if it held life-affirming liquid. She looked at it longingly, but refrained from taking that first sip.

Instead, she protested, "But then you don't have one."

"I can get one from the coffee machine down the hall. As long as it's hot, that's all that matters. Besides—" he nodded at the container she was holding "—that's not my first one of the morning. And if it's all the same to you, I'd rather you had my coffee than I had your bullet lodged somewhere in my torso because you were half-asleep when the gun went off."

Having heard enough, she took a deep sip and then sighed contentedly. "And they said that chivalry was dead."

"They," Esteban replied as he headed out into the hallway to get a container of coffee to replace the one he'd just given her, "were right. This is a purely selfish move on my part. I figure I need to stay alive if I'm ever going to dance on Jorge Lopez's grave."

The name meant nothing to her, but she ventured a guess as he walked back into the room three minutes later. "Jorge Lopez. I take it that he's the one who runs the drug cartel."

"Yes, he is." The answer was automatic. And then the significance of her rhetorical question hit him. "What do you know about the cartel?" Esteban asked suspiciously, watching her closely.

Still cradling the cup in both hands, Kari realized that she might have slipped. Was she supposed to know the drug lord's name or not? She hated playing games like this.

Kari shrugged in response to his question.

"Same thing that everyone else does," she answered. "That the cartel is evil and should be eradicated before all those vulnerable kids wind up either dead or getting hooked—or both."

She'd almost blown it, Kari upbraided herself. She hadn't made up her mind yet whether to tell him that she knew about his family and offer her condolences, or to just continue playing it by ear for the time being.

For now, she went with the latter.

"Why do you ask?" Kari said innocently.

His eyes held hers for a long, penetrating moment before he looked away. "No reason. Just thought maybe you'd heard something."

She decided to push it a little further, since that

was what she would have done under normal circumstances. "Like what?"

"Like me getting back undercover."

He really wanted that, didn't he? She felt bad for him. But she also knew that saying so was the fastest way of getting her head handed to her.

So instead, she cracked, "And give up this glamorous life where you can shower, shave and put on clean clothes in the morning? Surely you're kidding."

"Yeah," he muttered, his voice a monotone. "Dunno what I must have been thinking. So why did you stay here?" he asked. She hadn't given him an answer yet.

"I don't know," she admitted. "I thought that maybe if I stared at that board hard enough, and it was quiet enough, something I'd missed before might just come to me."

He looked at her, mildly interested as he sampled his coffee from the vending machine. It was particularly bitter—but not particularly hot. It was hard not making a face.

"And did it?"

"Yeah—that I still have no idea what the connection is between these two victims." There was frustration evident in her voice. "What we need," she told him, "is more data to work with."

"Maybe there doesn't have to be a connection," he suggested, setting the offending container of coffee down on his desk. "Maybe the killer just doesn't like nice, retired people who try to make a difference.

Maybe seeing them go about their lives makes him feel worse about himself."

Kari looked at him, impressed. But then, she recalled, he'd struck her as being smart back in high school. A jock who not only actually studied for exams—but who did well on them.

"That sounds very philosophical," she told him with a smile.

Esteban tossed off her compliment with an indifferent shrug. "Psych 101."

"Hey, Hyphen, Fernandez...get in here." Lieutenant Morrow stepped out of his office and called out to them.

Kari pulled herself up to her feet, waiting for the drained feeling to leave her. She handed Esteban back his coffee container. It was still half-full.

"Thanks," she told him, nodding at the container. And then she indicated the lieutenant, who'd already gone back into his office and was waiting for them to follow. "I don't think I like the sound of that."

Esteban said nothing. Taking the container back, he left it on his desk standing next to its smaller, rejected brethren, and followed behind Kari to the lieutenant's office.

Morrow didn't bother closing the door, giving them the impression that they weren't going to be in there all that long.

The impression was right.

"You got another one," he announced the second Esteban was in the office.

She didn't have to ask what he meant by "another one," because she knew. Still, she could hope that he was wrong. "You sure it's our guy?" Kari asked.

The look he gave her said he hadn't gotten to where he was by making mistakes. "It's him, all right. Throat slashed from behind."

Kari asked the next logical question, since she was trying to establish just what the killer's M.O. was. "Retired?"

Morrow looked at her, a puzzled furrow stretched across his brow. "What?"

"The victim," Kari underscored. "Was she—?"

"He," Morrow corrected.

Esteban surprised her by picking up the thread and asking the lieutenant, "Was he retired?"

The lieutenant shook his head. "Some of his co-workers found him at work when they came in this morning. That'll give them nightmares for a long time," he speculated. "He was an accountant," Morrow added, then produced the all-important slip of paper and held it out to Kari. "Here's the address."

Kari looked it over before sliding the paper into her pocket. She really should have gone home last night and gotten a decent night's sleep. That would have helped her more than finding out about Steve's— Esteban's—past, she told herself.

With a sigh, she looked in her partner's direction. "Okay, let's go."

"Why the long face?" he asked as they walked out of the lieutenant's office. "You said you wanted more data," he reminded her. They stopped at her desk so she could pick up her purse.

She did and they were on their way. Only then did she answer his question.

"I meant more data about the other two victims. I didn't want a third body to turn up." That was the *last* thing she had wanted.

"Maybe you should have been more specific," he told her.

Aghast, she shot him a look as they waited for the elevator to arrive. "What are you suggesting…that there's a serial killer fairy or a homicide genie out there, granting me three wishes?"

The elevator arrived and they got on. Since there was no one else in it, they continued talking. "No, just something more along the lines of 'careful what you wish for,'" he answered.

She was just punchy enough to see the merit in his argument. That alone convinced her that she needed more sleep.

"Well, if I did have three wishes…" she began.

"Yeah?" God help him, he *was* actually curious. Was this woman getting to him after all? He was going to have to watch that, not let himself risk opening up to her. You never knew who was listening, he thought.

"I'd wish my partner talked more to me."

That made him laugh. "Again, careful what you wish for," he warned.

"Why? Because you're going to turn into a chatterbox and talk my ear off?" Now *that* was funny, she thought. "There's more of a chance of me sprouting wings and flying—or our serial killer turning himself in and making a full confession," she tossed in, "than you suddenly running off at the mouth."

She had that pegged right, Esteban thought. "Hey, I've got an idea—why don't you just enjoy the peace and quiet?" he suggested.

She pretended it was an honest question and gave him an honest answer. "Because peace and quiet make me nervous," she admitted.

He laughed dryly, thinking she was joking. But one look at her face and he could see that she wasn't. "That's a new one."

She could see by Esteban's expression that he didn't believe her. Having nothing to lose, she decided to set him straight.

"No, really," she insisted. "When my surroundings are peaceful and quiet, I know that it's just a matter of time before something happens to shatter that…and at least half the time, what shatters peace and quiet is really not a good thing."

They got out on the ground floor and began walking to the exit and the parking lot beyond.

"So you catch yourself waiting and holding your

breath until whatever you know is going to happen—" she paused, then said "—happens."

In a way, they weren't all that different, always expecting some sort of chaos, Esteban thought. That was the way he lived his life, as well.

"Easy to peg you for a Cavanaugh," he commented. "Your family's always in the thick of it, all that constant action," he added in case she wasn't following his reasoning.

"We like keeping busy and keeping the peace," she told him.

"Or being in the middle of all the noise," he countered, giving the general situation another interpretation.

She inclined her head, not seeing the need to challenge the point he'd just made.

"There's that, too."

Unlike the other two victims, the third victim—a Ronald Hays—was in his early forties and, according to the coworker that they interviewed, Hays was far too busy with his social life to volunteer for any sort of activity. "Don't get me wrong—when they passed the hat around for Vera, Ron gave just like everyone else. Maybe even a little more," he added after thinking it over.

"Vera?" Kari asked, waiting for some kind of an explanation from the man who claimed to be the deceased's closest friend at the accounting firm.

The interviewee nodded. "Vera Wells," he clarified, but the name still didn't mean anything to her. "Vera's husband was in a car accident, and the bills just went through the roof in record time. We took up a collection in the office to help her cover a little of what the insurance didn't. Ron didn't even stop to count what he was putting in," he told them proudly, "just grabbed a handful of bills out of his wallet and slipped them all into the collection envelope.

"But he didn't have time for stuff like coaching some Little League team or mentoring a kid having trouble in his math class." The man laughed to himself as he recalled a specific incident.

"Remember something funny?" Esteban asked him.

The question, coming from someone like Esteban, instantly sobered the man being interviewed.

"Hell, when Ron got that jury summons in the mail, it put him in a bad mood for a week—especially when the boss told him his pay wasn't getting docked, that the company looked favorably on that sort of thing."

"Wait." Kari held up her hand, trying to understand. "You're saying he became angry because his pay *wasn't* getting docked?"

"Yeah. He was going to use that not-getting-paid thing as an excuse for getting out of jury duty. But since the boss said it was his patriotic duty to go down for jury duty, he had to go. And he wound up getting put on a case, too." The man paused to laugh, shaking his head as he began relaying more things about the incident. "I can tell you that *really* got him mad.

"Turns out, the case didn't last all that long. It started to, but Ron told me he pushed through the deadlock, convincing everyone else that the guy was guilty. They voted to convict the guy and Ron high-tailed it back to work.

"But you see, he just didn't have time for volunteering and selfless stuff like that." As if suddenly aware of the picture he'd just painted of the victim, the man's friend quickly added, "But that really didn't make him a bad guy."

"No," Kari agreed. "It didn't."

But what did? she couldn't help wondering. What made Ronald Hays, Mae Daniels and William Reynolds "bad guys," at least in the killer's eyes?

That, she thought, was the question that needed answering.

Chapter 11

The more she and Esteban delved into Ron Hays's life, the less he appeared to have in common with the first two victims. He was younger than they were, still employed and obviously had little interest in volunteering any of his free time to help those less fortunate than himself.

Kari paced back and forth in front of the bulletin board. Hays's photograph had been added to the board, taking its position next to William Reynolds and Mae Daniels.

Even the photograph looked out of place, Kari thought, slanting a glance toward it as she paced. Hays looked young enough to be their son.

Why was he victim number three?

Was he victim number three? she suddenly wondered, stopping dead in front of the board and staring at the man's photograph.

Leaning back in his chair, Esteban noted the way she was looking at the board—as if her eyes could shoot laser beams out. "Got something?" he asked.

Maybe yes, maybe no, she thought.

"Maybe someone killed Hays after reading about the other two murders," she theorized. She turned to look at her partner, her eyes bright.

Damn, but they were hypnotic, he thought. Like the rest of her. He forced himself to focus on her train of thought. "You mean, using the so-called serial killer—"

"*Almost* serial killer," Kari interjected. "Technically, it takes three like murders before we can call the perp a serial killer, and we haven't quite put Hays in the same category as Reynolds and Daniels," she reminded Esteban.

"Okay." He had no problem with adjusting his statement to suit her. He was accustomed to rolling with the punches—*most* of the time. "Using the so-called 'almost serial killer' for cover, whoever killed Ron Hays might have just been focused on getting rid of him and was hoping the murder wouldn't wind up on his doorstep." As he spoke, another idea occurred to him. "Or the other two murders he committed could

have been done to provide his cover and his real intended victim was Ron Hays all along," he suggested.

He watched her face to see her reaction, not quite
sure just what to expect. What he saw was an amused,
nonjudgmental smile. A smile that caught him a little
off guard. "What?" he demanded.

She would have never believed it. "You were a fan
of Agatha Christie mysteries when you were a kid,
weren't you?"

Defensiveness had always been second nature to
him. Now was no different. "What makes you say
that?" he wanted to know.

"Because you just described the setup behind one
of her classic stories. I think it was called *The ABC
Murders*. A killer murders three people in order to
'hide in plain sight' his intended victim."

Esteban frowned. "I take it you don't agree with
the last theory."

"I didn't say that," she pointed out. "I don't have
enough information on the third victim to rule that
'hide in plain sight' theory in or out right now." She
took a breath. "What I am saying is that the only thing
that we know for certain that victim number three has
in common with numbers one and two is that slashed
throat."

"Not the only thing."

Kari and Esteban turned around in unison and
looked toward the doorway at the woman who'd just

spoken. Sean's senior assistant, Destiny, was standing in the room.

"Okay," Esteban said gamely, recognizing the woman from the last crime scene. She'd been one of the investigators there. "What else is there?"

Kari looked at her hopefully. "You found something," she added, mentally crossing her fingers.

Destiny didn't answer either one of them. "The boss wants to see the two of you in his lab."

Kari knew better than to try to badger an answer out of Destiny. The woman could give lessons to clams when it came to being closemouthed.

"Lead the way," Kari told the other woman, gesturing toward the door.

Destiny wordlessly turned on her heel and did just that.

"You know, I don't recall you ever being this dramatic," Kari told her father as she and Esteban filed into the main lab directly behind Destiny.

Her father was there, along with his array of the latest state-of-the-art equipment, all of which was lined up along the dark blue granite counter within easy reach. When she spoke, Sean Cavanaugh looked up from the microscope he'd been using.

"Must have something to do with my renewed lease on life," her father speculated. He was all but beaming.

She noted that he'd been that way for weeks, ever

since Deirdre Callaghan had accepted his marriage proposal.

"Remind me to thank your fiancée the next time I see her," Kari told him, doing her best to look serious. About to say something else, she abruptly stopped as she remembered. "That'll be a week from Saturday, won't it? Boy, that came fast. I'm still trying to get used to the idea."

Because she could see from the slightly puzzled frown on Esteban's face that he wasn't following any of this, she told him, "My father's getting married next Saturday. To Detective Matt Callaghan's mother."

He was only vaguely aware of who Matt Callaghan was. He was still trying to become familiar with the names of various police detectives.

"Congratulations," Esteban said.

"Thanks." For a moment, Sean stepped outside his position as head of the lab and smiled at Esteban. "Why don't you come to the ceremony? Everyone's invited."

"I doubt if *everyone's* invited," Esteban responded, then saw by the expression on Kari's face that, just possibly, his assumption was inaccurate.

That seemed impossible…and yet, from what he'd picked up around town, the Cavanaughs were an extremely outgoing family—

Kari laughed at her partner. "Obviously, you haven't heard about the famous Andrew Cavanaugh get-togethers. I'm beginning to think the man is a direct descendent of one of those characters out of Aesop's fables, the one who had a jug that was never empty, no matter how much you poured out of it, and a basket that never ran out of bread, no matter how many loaves you removed from it."

Totally confused now, he looked at Sean for some sort of an explanation. "Is she going to start making sense soon?"

"Actually, she is making sense in her own way," Sean replied with a laugh. "It seems that for some reason, my brother knows how to whip up food for the masses without breaking a sweat. I've seen it for myself. No matter how many people turn up for an occasion, no one *ever* goes away from his door hungry, or thirsty—or disappointed, for that matter," he added with a smile.

"And he just *lives* for birthdays, weddings and christenings," Destiny chimed in.

"And whatever you do," Kari told him with a great deal of enthusiasm, "you really *don't* want to miss out on one of his Christmas celebrations."

The day held no special allure for him, or any special significance anymore. To Esteban, Christmas had become just another day, like all the other days that came before it and all the days that came after. But he instinctively knew that his opinion would not exactly go over well with these people, so he kept it to himself and merely asked, "Why?"

It was Sean who answered him. "Because Andrew

really pulls out all the stops. That includes coming up with new recipes, new ideas. Everything to make the holiday even bigger and better than the year before. I haven't been a member of the family for all that long, but I've never known him to disappoint."

"Wait, aren't you a Cavanaugh?" Esteban asked. "The former chief of police's younger brother?"

At least, that was what he'd heard—not that he paid strict attention to anything that wasn't directly related to his own survival. But everyone seemed to either be friends with a Cavanaugh or have a story about them.

"Yes, but due to a mix-up at the hospital many years ago, I came on the scene rather late," Sean explained.

Kari saw the befuddled expression whisper across Esteban's ruggedly handsome features before it disappeared. He had obviously learned to keep his thoughts locked away for the most part. She leaned over in his direction and murmured, "I'll explain later."

The promise intrigued him. Her breath, warm and enticing along his cheek and neck, intrigued him more. He succeeded in keeping his reaction from being evident. No one looking at him would have guessed that he was actually reacting to the woman next to him rather than listening to the man standing in front of him.

"But I didn't call you both down here to talk about my pending nuptials," Sean announced, suddenly looking serious again. "The M.E. finished his preliminary exam and thought you might be interested in seeing what he found folded up and stuffed into the victim's mouth."

"His mouth?" Kari echoed. "The killer put something into Hays's mouth?" The guy really was sick, she thought. "Why?"

"It'll make more sense once you see *what* he stuffed into the victim's mouth," her father promised. So saying, he produced an eight-by-eleven flat plastic envelope. Inside was a colorful sheet that had obviously been torn out of a magazine. The page had been crumpled and some of the wording was ruined because of moisture, most likely saliva.

"My best guess would be that it was an act of hostility," Sean told them.

"An act of hostility," Esteban repeated. "You mean over and above savagely slashing the guy's throat?" he asked.

Sean chuckled to himself. "Point taken. We're dealing with one very angry individual," he told the two detectives as he nodded at the sealed piece of evidence.

"So you *do* think it's the same guy," Kari said, watching her father's face.

Sean indicated the magazine page on the table with his eyes. "What do you think?"

Kari looked down at the photograph on the magazine page. Though not as clear as it could have been because of the damage done by the saliva, it was a photograph of a Greek goddess holding up the scales of justice.

"Well, it's official," Kari sighed.

Esteban quirked a dark brow in her direction. "What is?"

"Our guy's a serial killer. Three's the magic number. And this makes three." She looked at her father. "Anything else?"

"Not right now," he answered. Kari turned toward Esteban. "Okay, back to the drawing board," she said, resigned. "See you later, Dad. Destiny—" She gestured toward the young woman.

Esteban said nothing, only nodded at the head of the lab before falling into step beside Kari as they retraced their steps back to the squad room.

Only when they had gotten back to their desks and to the bulletin board that was the source of frustration to them both did he finally say anything at all.

"Maybe there's something in the third victim's life that'll lead us back to the other two."

Kari's mouth dropped open as she looked at him in surprise. "That's the most optimistic thing I think I've heard you say so far. Way to go," she said, cheering him on.

He was afraid of that. He'd noticed that she had a habit of expecting more of the same once something went her way.

"Yeah, well, don't get used to it," he warned.

"I'll try to contain myself," she promised, not even bothering to try to hide her amused grin. And then, after a beat, she decided to do a little reinforcement. "He was serious, you know."

He was busy trying to put the pieces together and her comment came out of nowhere, disorienting him. "Who was serious about what?"

"My father. About inviting you to the wedding," she reiterated.

His brows drew together. She was kidding, right? "Why would your father, the head of the department's crime lab, want me at his wedding?"

"Why not?" Kari countered. He still didn't get it, did he? Her family didn't operate by the usual rules. They made friends, not acquaintances—especially when it appeared that a person needed a friend.

"Because he doesn't know me from Adam," Esteban emphasized. That seemed like more than enough reason to him.

"I think he knows you a little better than that," Kari said. "Besides, you're my partner. That's enough for my father." She searched his face, trying to see if any of this was getting through to him. How closed off *was* this man, anyway? "Didn't anyone tell you that we're all one big, happy family here?"

"I must have missed that memo," he snickered. He didn't want to get pulled in with these people. Something told him that there was a chance they could actually get to him, actually form a crack in his wall. Which was dangerous. Because cracks allowed things to seep in—and inevitably, that left room for colossal pain. He'd been there, done that.

He didn't want to go through it again.

"Well, I'm giving you the audio version," Kari informed him. "The police department is actually one big family and the Cavanaughs are considered a subset of that. Although, to be honest, I think we'd probably be one big, happy family even if we were a bunch of farmers and *not* part of the police department." She added speculatively, "But being part of law enforcement probably works better for us…." Finished for the moment, she waited for Esteban to respond. When he didn't, she had no choice but to press, "So, is that a yes?"

His thoughts already elsewhere, he looked at her distractedly. "Yes to what?"

"You have *got* to do something about your attention span, Fernandez," she insisted. "You sound like a husband in training." She reworded her question more completely, enunciating each word. "Are you going to come to my father's wedding next Saturday?"

She wasn't going to give him any peace until he agreed, although why it mattered to her one way or another he hadn't a clue. Still, to get a little respite he said, "Yeah, sure, why not?"

It was the kind of answer that someone gave when they meant no but didn't want to get into a discussion over it, Kari thought. She was not about to let the matter drop. "You want me to pick you up?"

Esteban switched tactics. "Why? You don't trust me to show up?"

She thought about denying the truth, about letting all this go for the time being. But that only meant that the subject had to be revisited at some point—and since they weren't getting anywhere with the serial killer investigation at the moment, she wanted to be able to clear up at least this one thing.

Besides, they could use the break. Or at least she could, she amended.

"Actually, no, I don't," she admitted.

He went on the offensive. There apparently was no other way with this woman, he thought.

"What does it matter to you if I show up or not?" he wanted to know.

The look in her eyes told him she was digging in. For a gorgeous woman, she could be one hell of a pain in the butt. Why that would make her even more attractive to him was a mystery he didn't think he could solve.

"Because I think it would do you good," she said.

"And you know this for a fact," he jeered.

Kari held her ground, raising her chin defiantly. "Pretty much."

Her chin made for one hell of a tempting target. Lucky for her, she was a female. Not so lucky for him. "How?" he challenged.

"Because, like that old song said, people need people. Socializing is healthy," she insisted when he waved a dismissive hand at her and turned away. She sidestepped him and literally got into his face again. "It forces you to get outside yourself and talk to people, instead of just dwelling on whatever it is that's bothering you."

What was bothering him was her, and right now there seemed to be no way around that. Maybe he should have stayed underground and taken his chances with the cartel. At least death would have been reasonably quick, without any of this subtle torture he kept encountering.

"I had no idea you had a degree in psychology," he grumbled.

She didn't bat an eye, or rise to the insult she knew he meant to get under her skin.

"I don't. I have a degree in people. When you grow up around six brothers and sisters, you tend to pick up a few things—unless, of course, you're a rock."

And she, he caught himself thinking as his eyes slid over the damnably soft, inviting curves of her body, was as far from being a rock as possible.

"I'd said I'd be there," he reminded her.

"And I said that I'd pick you up."

"You don't have to go through that trouble," he reiterated through gritted teeth. "Just give me the address where all this is taking place."

"No trouble," she stubbornly assured him, not giving an inch.

"You don't trust me," he accused again. They'd

come full circle in less than five minutes, he couldn't help thinking.

She smiled complacently at him, forbidding her headache to move forward. She needed to win this argument. "No further than I can throw you—and I'm strong, but not nearly *that* strong," she told him.

This was getting him nowhere and he had no idea how long he could resist wrapping his hands around her pretty little neck—or wrapping them around other parts of her delectable anatomy, for that matter. For some reason, verbal confrontations just upped the stakes and made him want her more.

He nodded toward the bulletin board. "Why don't we get back to what they're paying us for?"

"Good point," she answered. Break was over, time to get on with it.

Putting her thinking cap back on, she took in a deep breath, scrutinizing the bulletin board. "Okay, from the top," she announced. "We're going to see if we can find something else that these three people had in common. The same club, the same church, the same doctor—there has to be *some* kind of a tie. Since God knows they don't look alike, the killer's not picking them because they're a certain type."

"Sounds like that means a lot of banging on closed doors," he commented.

Kari arched a brow. "I thought you were the one who liked doing legwork," she couldn't help reminding him.

"Alone," he told her. "I like doing it alone."

Her smile never faded. "Well, we can't all have what we want. The trick is to want what you have."

He stared at her. That sounded like some sort of brain teaser. "What's that supposed to mean?"

"Think on it, Fernandez," she told him cheerfully. "Tell me what you come up with."

Suppressing a groan, Esteban raked a hand through his hair. He didn't know which was worse. That she tempted him or that she was driving him crazy. "I'll tell you what I come up with—that I need a new partner."

She pretended to gasp in surprise. "I thought you didn't want a partner."

"I don't, but if I have to have one—" He wouldn't give her up and he knew it. "Oh, the hell with it." There was no point in trying to work out a run-of-the-mill truce. That was for ordinary people, and if there was one thing that this woman fate had saddled him with wasn't, it was ordinary. "Tell me what you want me to do."

She grinned broadly. "Music to my ears, Esteban." He had a feeling he'd just made a fatal error.

And there was no turning back.

Chapter 12

Doing her very best to ignore the annoying butter-flies that had come out of nowhere and were currently dive-bombing inside her stomach, Kari was just about to hurry out her front door when she noticed how loose her left shoe felt. With a sigh, she dropped her purse on the floor, bent over and paused to adjust the buckle on her high-heeled sandals. If she didn't, she just *knew* there would be a pratfall in her future, most likely right in front of her dour partner.

It was a week and a half later, and their investiga-tion into the slasher murders was at a standstill, but at least no more bodies had turned up. So, just for today, the day of her father's wedding, she was putting everything else on the back burner and just focusing on the celebration ahead.

If she hadn't paused, she would have missed it. Missed the message that had all but silently crept onto the screen of her cell phone. Unlike an incoming call, which would have been fairly audible, the whisper-soft text message alert would have gone completely unnoticed once she was inside her car, driving toward the hub of all Cavanaugh activity…otherwise known as Uncle Andrew's house.

And she wouldn't have known.

With all the excitement of the day, she would have just assumed that Esteban had gotten lost in the crowd—and it was an irrefutable fact that when the Cavanaughs all got together, they most definitely did comprise a crowd. There were enough of them to populate their own small town.

In addition to family, her father and his bride-to-be had invited a ton of friends to the ceremony and reception, as well. There were absolutely enough people to form a small village. Perhaps even a medium-size one.

But fortunately, Kari *had* stopped to struggle with an uncooperative ankle strap, which was why she was able to hear the buzzing sound that told her she had a new text message.

The strap now sufficiently tightened, Kari picked up her small purse and began to dig through it, searching for her cell phone. As it turned out, the phone was playing hide-and-seek behind her wallet and under her rather large set of keys.

Taking it out, she brought up the screen and saw the no-frills, stripped-bare message: *Changed my mind.*

That was it. Three words. End transmission.

Vague though the words were in nature, she didn't even have to look to see who had sent the message. She knew. It had come from her definitely *un*-loquacious partner, Esteban.

The message could only mean that he had changed his mind about coming to the wedding.

"No, you didn't," she informed the cell phone with finality, throwing it back into her purse.

Kari decided not to waste any time calling him and arguing about his reversal in plans over the phone. This was something she felt could be far better handled in person. So, locking up her house, she got into her car and drove like a woman possessed to his home. She was fairly certain that Esteban thought that since he'd sent this message so late and she was probably a typical female who needed absolutely every second she could spare to get ready for the wedding, there wouldn't be any time to come get him.

"Wrong," she announced rather loudly to the absent Fernandez. "Obviously the man does *not* know who he is dealing with."

Kari absolutely hated waiting for people and, consequently, she was never late herself. Being on time was practically a second religion for her.

She was also grateful that she'd had the foresight to have gotten Esteban's address from Brenda that first day her uncle had made them partners. Otherwise, she would have been really hard-pressed to rectify this situation…as she fully intended to do.

Making all the lights—some just barely—Kari managed to get to Esteban's garden apartment complex in just over seven minutes flat. She'd driven all the way keeping one eye open for any overzealous patrol officers who might have taken exception to the mileage she was covering in an exceedingly short amount of time.

But she didn't want to miss the ceremony, and she *didn't* want Esteban to spend the day inhabiting the dark corners that she knew in her heart he had created for himself. The very best cure for that that she knew of, from all that she'd gleaned thus far, was exposure to the various members of the multigenerational Cavanaugh family. They had cornered the market on well-being and happiness, and they were more than willing to share the wealth. In fact, they acted as if it was their duty to share.

She had already discovered for herself that attending one of these family functions literally left no place to hide. No matter where a person might turn, there were Cavanaughs *everywhere*.

Kari smiled to herself. "You're not winning this one, Fernandez. Even if I have to drag you there kicking and screaming, it'll be for your own good in the long run. You'll thank me for it someday."

If worst came to worst, she knew that she could always call in one of her brothers to lend his muscle to the cause.

But she didn't want it to come to that. What she really wanted was to be able to handle this on her own, to keep this just between her and Esteban. The ball, though, was in her partner's court and it all depended on how bullheaded he intended to be.

Because no matter how stubborn a jackass Esteban was planning on being, she fully intended to outmaneuver him.

When Esteban heard the doorbell, he ignored it. Ignored it the first time it rang, as well as the second time.

And the third.

But the ringing noise was definitely getting on his nerves and he crossed to the door. He was pretty sure he knew who was on the other side of it and he was going to demand to know why the hell she couldn't take no for an answer.

He had his hand on the doorknob when the door suddenly opened, all but hitting him right in the stomach.

Jumping back, out of the door's range, he went for his service revolver before remembering that he'd left it on the top shelf of his hall closet.

The next second, he saw that he really didn't need his gun—unless, of course, he used it to put himself out of his misery…which at this point seemed like a viable possibility.

"How did you get in?" he demanded, glaring at Kari and trying not to notice that the silver cocktail dress she had on made her look sexier than should have been legally allowed. "I locked the door."

She merely smiled complacently at him and said, "One of the perks of coming from a large family of law enforcement agents. You learn a lot of useful miscellaneous information that might come in handy at some point," she told him.

"Like breaking and entering?" he challenged, because that was clearly what she'd just done to gain access to his apartment.

"Were you going to open the door for me? I did ring," she pointed out pleasantly. She already knew that he hadn't been about to let her in, but she wanted to hear what he had to say on the matter.

He looked away, a disgruntled expression on his handsome face. The man really should smile more, she thought. When he did, he looked almost exactly the way he had when he'd been a high school heartthrob.

"I didn't hear you. I must have been out of hearing range," he said.

"Where?" she wanted to know. "On the moon? Because I rang loud enough for the next county to hear me. Never mind," she cut him off before he could attempt to stitch together some sort of lame excuse. "That's all behind us. I'm here now and I'm going to take you to the wedding. Get dressed," she ordered, then forced a wide smile on her face in hope that it might help in moving him along.

It didn't.

Esteban looked down at the jeans and T-shirt he had on. "I wasn't aware that I was naked."

Trust him to go that route. His flippant comment instantly created an image of just that in her mind. The dive-bombing butterflies turned into dive-bombing Boeing jets. With that picture in her head, she found breathing to be rather challenging.

Finally, despite a bone-dry tongue, Kari managed to say, "You want to go like that, fine with me." She shrugged indifferently. "Let's go."

But Esteban remained exactly where he was. "You're missing the point," he informed her. "I do *not* want to go at all."

Her eyes darkened as they met his. "So let me get this straight. You're refusing to go."

"So you *do* understand English," he declared triumphantly. "I was beginning to worry."

"Yes, I do." Her eyes remained unwaveringly on his. "The question is, do *you* understand the consequences arising out of this little rebellious stand of yours."

"Absolutely. I get to spend a quiet day here—starting when you walk out the door." He held it open for her, waiting for Kari to take his blatant hint and finally leave.

Two could stand fast, she thought, calmly adding, "But there's more."

He should have known, Esteban thought irritably. A skin rash was easier to get rid of than this woman. He didn't know whether the fact that she was so damn attractive made it better or worse to endure this ridiculous standoff.

"More?" he questioned.

"Yes, more. More consequences," she emphasized, then spelled it out for him, tackling one section at the time so that it could really sink in. "Like the fact that by not showing up after receiving an official invitation from one of the main participants of this event, you are in effect insulting approximately half the Aurora Police Department, not to mention the Chief of Detectives—never a good career move," she underscored, then continued, "the former chief of police *and* the head of the daytime CSI unit, who also happens to be the bridegroom. Do you *really* want to do that?" she asked Esteban, pinning him with a piercing look.

He bit back a few choice words that rose to his lips. Instead, he sighed melodramatically and said, "Did anyone ever tell you that you were one hell of a giant pain in the butt?"

She surprised him by saying, "Actually, yes, they have, but seeing as how the person saying that was one of my brothers and I had just won an argument at the time, I didn't let it faze me much. A little like right now," she added pointedly.

They were running out of time. She proceeded to wrap it all up. "Now then, if you can change your clothes fast, I'll wait. If you can't, then this just turned into a come-as-you-are event and we're leaving right now. The family doesn't really care that much about what a person wears, anyway. I just thought that you might." Kari paused for her words to sink in, then asked, "So what'll it be?"

He answered her question with a question. So far, she'd managed to counter him at every turn. Was she just lucky—or very good? He held off on final judgment. "There's no third option?"

She pretended to think for a second. "There's my dragging you to the ceremony kicking and screaming, but that's really a last resort and, all things being equal, I'd rather not have to do that."

The woman thought a lot of her abilities, he mused. She had to have a pretty inflated sense of self. "You really think you could?" he taunted with a dismissive laugh.

Her eyes remained locked on his and her expression didn't change an iota. Nonetheless, there was something almost chilling about it, Esteban thought.

"This is the part," she was saying to him, "where my brothers—and father—would firmly suggest that you not test me."

She *had* to be kidding. "I far outweigh you and I'm

practically a foot taller," Esteban reminded her. At this point he was more amused by her bravado than anything else.

She looked at him coolly. "It's not about size. It's about leverage—and opportunity."

Now, that was a crock, he thought.

"And just what's that supposed to— Hey!"

Esteban had no time to even frame his question. The next instant, the air had gone flying out of his lungs. Catching him completely by surprise, Kari had swung around, twisted his arm behind his back and successfully brought Esteban down to his knees.

There was actually searing pain shooting through his arm and shoulder, and he found himself stunned, immobilized and, he had to admit, somewhat impressed by the pint-size woman with the iron grip.

Gritting his teeth together to keep the pain from emerging in grunts and half gasps, Esteban ground out, "All right. If it means so much to you, I'll go."

"Good." She released her hold on his arm and took a step back. "I'm taking you at your word. Just remember, I can always do that again."

Not twice, you can't, he silently promised her. But there was time for that—and for evening the score— later. But right now, he inclined his head and said, "Give me a minute then."

She could have before, but she couldn't now. Not if they were going to make the ceremony despite any traffic snarls. "Sorry, you already used that up. Just grab a sports jacket, if you have one, out of your closet and let's go," she instructed in a no-nonsense voice that matched her expression. "I hate being late."

"Then by all means, go on ahead," he suggested amicably, gesturing toward his front door. "I'll take my car."

Did he think she was born half an hour ago? She was not about to take her eyes off the elusive Fernandez.

"No," Kari informed him sternly, "you won't. And what kind of fool do you take me for? Now, if you don't want to grab a jacket, that's fine, too. But you *are* coming with me to the wedding."

Resigned, Esteban paused to grab a dress jacket from his hall closet, then led the way out his front door, since he could see that pretending to follow her out just wasn't going to fly with this woman.

"Have you ever given a thought to being a dominatrix?" he wanted to know, slanting a glance in her direction to see her reaction to the question. He reasoned that she would either display a sense of humor—or an offended sense of morality.

Kari never blinked. "Maybe as a second career option after I retire from the force."

Esteban laughed in response. It was the kind of laugh back then that had instantly caught her attention and had gone a long way to captivating her heart, as well. Infectious, compelling, genuine, it was a sound that a person couldn't remain indifferent to.

She'd made a breakthrough, Kari thought, silently congratulating herself. A breakthrough that allowed her to bridge the past and the present for her reluctant partner.

She felt like cheering.

"Where'd you learn that move you used on me in the apartment?" he asked her out of the blue as she started her car.

Since she was watching the road, he only saw her profile, but he could make out the corner of her mouth curving. What he saw of the smile was enough to rope him in.

He found himself being tantalized. Against his will, he recalled the way her mouth felt against his that night she came bearing whiskey and arguments.

"I could answer that," she told him. "But then I'd have to kill you."

Esteban surprised her by saying, "It might be worth it."

It wasn't a secret, really—just something she had picked up a few years back and never forgotten. It was the kind of move that gave you confidence and made you feel less vulnerable in the world.

"I went to college with this girl who came from Israel. Shula's whole family was either in the military or involved in an agency that was her country's equivalent of our CIA. She was the only girl, and her father, uncles and brothers were very protective of her. They taught her all sorts of things she could use to stay safe. She passed some of those maneuvers on to me," she explained.

"And did she?" Esteban asked her. "Stay safe?" he added when she didn't answer his question.

She'd lost touch with the dark-eyed young woman after graduation. Something she regretted, but it couldn't be helped. They both had lives waiting for them after graduation. Kari had always wanted to join the force, and Shula, most likely, was a spy by now.

"Last I heard," she said.

"So you have any more moves I should know about?" Esteban asked wryly.

This time, she spared him a look and smiled.

He found her smile not just intriguing, but pretty damn compelling. If he didn't know better, he would have said he could feel himself being reeled in.

And resistance, he discovered, as the saying went, was futile.

"I have lots of moves, Fernandez. Cross me and you'll find out just how many," she promised in a voice that might have been used to describe a favorite episode of a beloved television series.

"I'll pass," he responded, adding, "maybe some other time. But right now I have this wedding I'm supposed to be attending."

Kari grinned, relieved that her stubborn partner had apparently finally made his peace with coming to her father's wedding. And she hadn't even had to hog-tie him. She supposed this was progress.

"Yes," she agreed, "you do."

They turned down a long tree-lined block. By their towering size, it was evident that the trees had been there a very long time.

"Hey, Hyphen," he said to her, "answer a question for me."

Inwardly, she braced herself, knowing that nothing was ever really easy with this man. She supposed that was what kept it interesting. "Shoot."

"If I still had refused to come with you, would you really have strong-armed me into coming?"

She looked at him out of the corner of her eye as she took another right turn. This one brought her onto one of the main thoroughfares that ran practically the length of Aurora and would eventually lead to her uncle's house.

"With my dying breath, Fernandez," she told him. "With my dying breath."

There wasn't a hint of a smile on her lips.

Suppressing a grin of his own, Esteban had a feeling that she was actually being serious.

Kari had obviously done a lot of growing up since she'd been that quiet girl with those mesmerizing eyes back in high school, he thought.

Who would have ever guessed?

Chapter 13

He was absorbed the moment he and Kari stepped over the threshold into the house already teeming with earlier arrivals.

There was no other way to describe what happened to him, except for that word.

Absorbed.

He wasn't prepared for it.

Esteban had spent so many years literally being on the outside while pretending to be someone he wasn't. The trouble was, he'd been that other "person" for so long and had done such a good, believable job of it—until someone had ratted him out—that now he wasn't sure how to be himself or even who that actually was.

Consequently, he entered the home of Andrew Cavanaugh without an identity intact.

And they accepted him anyway.

For the past couple of weeks or so, Esteban had worked among them—it was hard going anywhere in the station without tripping over a Cavanaugh—not to mention that the beguiling partner that had been thrust on him was one of them. But even so, coming to this wedding, he'd thought that he would be on the outside looking in. Just as usual.

Instead, he was immediately considered to be "in." Immediately accepted and welcomed.

Just like that.

Andrew Cavanaugh, the host of this major family event, had opened the door for them himself. After hugging Kari, the man unexpectedly clasped his hand and shook it heartily, his booming voice filling the foyer as he greeted him.

"So you're the new guy I've been hearing so much about." Then the former chief of police laughed, still holding Esteban's hand as he drew him into the house. "Don't look so worried, Detective. It's all good," Andrew assured the younger man.

"If you don't mind my asking, sir, who have you been hearing all this *from?*" Esteban asked.

Finally breaking the physical connection, Andrew merely smiled and said, "Reliable sources. That's all you need to know. Either of you," he added, his penetrating look sweeping over both his niece and her new partner.

"Go," he urged. "Get yourselves something to eat, something to drink, and mingle. The ceremony's going to start soon." He looked at Kari. "Your uncle's about ready to officiate. He's getting set up in the back." And then Andrew paused for a moment, looking pointedly at Esteban. "He might still need help with the altar," he speculated. His inference was clear: he wanted Esteban to pitch in and get involved.

"Altar?" Esteban asked, not quite sure he'd heard correctly.

Andrew nodded. "It's actually something some of the boys rigged up. Mostly it looks like a wooden arch with flowers woven through it," he told them. He gestured toward the back. "It's that way. I'll see you both out back for the ceremony," he said in parting.

Kari flashed her uncle a smile, then turned back to Esteban. "Guess we'd better go out back," she said before leading the way through the crowd.

The backyard, like the living room they had just threaded their way through, was a hive of activity in absolutely every direction. It was enough, Esteban thought, to make a man's head spin.

"One of your uncles is performing the wedding?" he asked her, somewhat surprised.

She nodded even as she scanned the area for the man in question. "My uncle Adam is a priest."

"A priest?" Esteban echoed, puzzled. "I thought

that all the Cavanaughs were involved in some area of law enforcement."

"You thought right," she confirmed. "They are, one way or another. My uncle Adam is a Cavelli," she told him, then went on to explain further. "That's the last name of the family my dad *thought* he belonged to. The family he grew up with. He thought he had four brothers and sisters—before he discovered he was a Cavanaugh. Now there are a lot more relatives."

The last sentence, in his opinion, was unnecessary. What *was* necessary was a way of identifying everyone. "How the hell do you tell who's who without some kind of a playbook or name-tag system?" he wanted to know, mystified as he looked around at all the different clusters of people scattered throughout the immediate area.

She laughed at the completely overwhelmed expression on Esteban's face. She had a feeling that there wasn't all that much that threw him for a loop, but her family obviously did.

"It does take a little time," she admitted. "But it's well worth the effort. I could see how it might be a little overwhelming for someone, though." She decided to give him an example to work with. "Think of it as the first day of college. You don't know anybody and it's intimidating. But after a couple of weeks, you start making friends and it begins to all fall into place. Pretty soon, you're in a comfortable niche."

"I'm not interested in a comfortable niche *or* in

making any friends," he informed her in a clipped voice. "I'm just interested in doing my job."

Kari abruptly stopped walking through the yard and looked at him as if she was certain she hadn't heard him correctly.

"Why wouldn't you want to make friends? It's very lonely without friends," she said. Then, picking up on the signs, she said quietly to him, "But I think you already know that."

"Hey, Steve—right?" Thomas, her oldest brother called out, waving at her partner to get his attention.

"Esteban," Esteban corrected him. His name hadn't been that important to him when he was younger. But it was now. Having lost everything else—his mother, his brother and, in part, his stepfather, since the man was now in prison serving twenty to life—his heritage was all that he had left, and Esteban was determined to hang on to it.

"Sorry. Esteban," Thomas acknowledged with a cheerful nod. "Need an opinion here," he told Kari's partner. "Tell me if I've finally got this damn thing level, will you?" he asked.

With a shrug, Esteban did as he was asked and with that one single, small action, he wound up shedding the last residual traces of being an outsider. He was part of them now, part of the brotherhood that made up the family of cops, as tightly connected a family as any in the annals of history.

If, during the course of the rest of the day and the

evening to follow, Esteban began to entertain ideas about pulling back, those notions were promptly smashed by one person or another.

Esteban found himself pulled into one conversation after another almost seamlessly. Each time he thought he was separating himself from one group, another group would snare him.

And, throughout it all, there was Kari. Kari, beside him at the wedding, quietly shedding tears of joy and getting his handkerchief damp. Kari, urging him to sample yet another dish of something he didn't recognize and bringing him a gin and tonic rather than a glass of champagne—which he loathed—so he could properly toast the new bride and groom.

And Kari, who wound up coaxing him onto the dance floor.

It seemed as if it had been an eternity since he'd had an occasion to dance—or the desire to.

The first time she threaded her hand through his and began pulling him toward the temporary dance floor that two of her cousins had constructed less than twenty-four hours before the wedding, he had dragged his feet, resisting.

"I'll step all over your feet," he'd protested, falling back on the age-old excuse.

"I really doubt that," she'd told him. Knowing she couldn't say she had seen him on the dance floor back in high school—he'd already denied that he was *that*

Steve Fernandez—she fell back on a small white lie. "You look like rhythm would come naturally to you."

He'd laughed shortly at that. "I think you have entirely too much faith in this overblown image you've conjured up of me."

Taking his left hand, Kari positioned it on her hip, then took his right hand in hers and drew him in closer to her.

A lot closer.

The air seemed to shift, bringing with it a wave of warmth that transcended anything the air-conditioning could negate—if there had been any out there, which there wasn't.

"I think, Esteban," she said, emphasizing his name, "you're completely up to anything I come up with— and more." Her eyes held his to make her point. "And you're right, I do have great faith in you…but I believe that faith's justified."

"Based on what?" he wanted to know.

As far as he knew, he hadn't done anything to prove himself to be an asset to her. Ordinarily, he wouldn't even want to. But of late there had started to be this small, nagging desire inside him. He wasn't even sure just what sort of desire was involved, just that it was there.

And it was growing.

"Gut instinct," she told him cheerfully. "Something you're born with if you're a Cavanaugh."

He pinned her with a look as their hips all but

locked in syncopated rhythm. "But you were born a Cavelli," he reminded her.

"That was a technicality that has since been smoothed out," she told him, unfazed. "And, for the record, I was right."

He felt as if they were in two different conversations—and he had lost track of hers. "Right about what?"

The tempo was slow. Her movements, slower. And sensual as hell. He was *really* doing his best not to notice, but it was like trying not to notice that he needed to breathe. It was damn impossible.

"About what I said when I dragged you out onto the dance floor earlier. I said you could dance and that's exactly what you're doing, you know. You're dancing. Dancing so well, other couples are stopping just to watch," she told him proudly.

That wasn't the only thing he was doing, Esteban thought.

In addition to dancing, he was feeling. Without any conscious consent on his part, he could feel parts of him that had been placed in frozen suspended animation suddenly thawing out.

That wasn't supposed to be happening.

He worked better the other way, when there was nothing distracting him, nothing to be aware of but the job and survival. Focusing on anything but bringing down the enemy just complicated things and got in the way of his functioning properly.

Got in the way of his being an asset to both the department and his partner.

He couldn't allow this to continue. Or worse, to grow. It had been a great day, one to someday look back on fondly, but it was time to end it, while he could still find his way back to the barren land he'd occupied for almost the past four years.

"I don't think this was such a good idea," he told her, his comment encompassing not just his dancing with her but the entire outing, as well.

But Kari wasn't ready to throw in the towel, wasn't ready to allow her common sense to take over and dictate her actions. Because, like a good detective, she knew she was traversing through dangerous terrain. But right now she was enjoying herself more than she was worried about the consequences of her actions. More than she was worried about the Pandora's box she'd just opened.

"I do," she told him, her voice barely above a whisper as her words and her breath seemed to seep in through his shirt and echo against his skin.

He found himself fighting it again, fighting the urge to kiss her the way he had that first night in his apartment, when she'd come over bearing a bottle of bourbon and pulled out all the stops to sway him into becoming her partner.

He'd kissed her then, he'd told himself, to scare her off. But it had backfired on him, not only failing to frighten her off, but also succeeding in introducing fear back into his own life. Fear that he was, despite all his best efforts to the contrary, vulnerable beneath all those hard layers of his.

And she had made him that way.

Kari could literally feel it, feel the tug-of-war he was going through, feel it because it was the very same tug-of-war that *she* was going through, as well.

She knew, without being subjected to a lecture, that getting involved with your partner in anything but a professional way was not exactly the smartest move a detective could make. Having romantic feelings clouded judgment and took the edge off reaction time, made you slower, caused you to hesitate a microsecond—just long enough to get you killed.

She'd heard stories to that effect time and again and knew it was true.

Knew too that right now she just didn't care. Because what was going on inside her had taken center stage and would continue to build steam until she experienced some form of release—and soon. And since she wasn't planning on bungee jumping off the Golden Gate Bridge anytime within the next couple of days, that really left her only one viable way out.

She wanted to be with him.

Wanted to be with this man who pretended not to know her, pretended not to remember her for whatever reason that suited him.

But denying the past didn't change it, didn't mean

it had never happened, no matter how much he wished it to the contrary.

But if it helped him get through his day and go on with his life, who was she to upset the balance he'd struck?

If he wanted her to know that he'd lied about who he was…that he *was* in fact the wildly popular high school jock who had inhabited the dreams of half the girls attending Aurora High all those years ago, then he would tell her in his own time. And she could wait, at least for that.

But as for waiting for him to make that first move, to lead her where she found herself so desperately wanting to go, well, that was another story. One that she might have to take upon herself to orchestrate if she wanted it to happen.

Even now she could feel every bone in her body growing tense and impatient.

She was going to have to do something about that, Kari thought—and taking an extralong, extracold shower tonight really didn't seem as though it would be the answer to her problem.

But for now she did her best to put a lid on it. After all, she reasoned, she couldn't very well jump him here, right in the middle of her father's wedding reception.

At the very least, she was going to have to wait until they were alone, and that wasn't going to happen until they left the party.

Laying her head against Esteban's shoulder, she went on dancing and just enjoyed his company as well as his close proximity.

For now that had to be enough.

As she was reining herself in, Esteban went on telling himself that his incredibly sexy partner wasn't distracting him, and that he *wasn't* experiencing any sort of longings, beyond wishing that the band would take a long break right about now so that he could cool off.

He was getting rather good at lying.

"Are they all like that?" Esteban asked her.

They had said their goodbyes and were almost at his apartment complex when he finally broached the question. It was several hours later, and even though the whole event had lasted more than twelve hours, he and Kari were hardly the last ones to leave when they'd finally decided it was time to go.

He'd been so quiet, she'd become convinced that Esteban wasn't going to talk at all. That maybe this was his way of handling the potent attraction that she'd felt growing between them. Because there was definitely something going on, and she was convinced that she wasn't the only one who felt it.

But she had also begun to think that Esteban's way of dealing with it was to slip into denial, and for him that seemed to mean silence.

It took her a second to run his question through her

head, and even then she couldn't make much sense of it.

"Huh? What are you talking about?" she asked him, confused.

"The Cavanaugh weddings." He reasoned that this couldn't have been the first one she'd attended, which meant that she had something to go by to make a judgment. "Are they all these marathon affairs?"

Now she understood his question. Looking at the situation from his point of view, she could see why he'd ask. He'd been a loner for too long and had no family to relate to anymore.

"Andrew Cavanaugh's shindigs, be they wedding ceremonies, birthday parties, Christmas celebrations or just spur-of-the-moment things he throws together, go on for at least half a day, if not more." Her mouth curved as she recalled one particular example. "When my branch of the family came to light, the party he threw began on a Friday afternoon and lasted until Sunday night. That's a family that likes each other's company," she told him with fondness in her voice. "The food, fabulous though it is, is secondary to the company—just don't tell Uncle Andrew I said so. He takes a great deal of pride in his cooking."

He lifted a brow. "And when would I get a chance to tell him that?"

She didn't even have to pause to think before she answered. "At the next party."

They were already planning another one? So soon? "I wasn't invited," he pointed out.

She realized that she needed to explain the rules to him. "Once you attend one party, the invitation is a standing one and understood. The only way to get out of the perpetual invitations is to die," she deadpanned. She saw his expression grow somber. "I'm sorry, did I say something wrong?"

Her question surprised him, catching him off guard. "What makes you say that?"

"Well, for one thing, you look like you're a million miles away." *For another,* she added silently, *you look sad.*

"No, I'm just remembering something." They had reached their destination and she parked in the last spot in guest parking. He blew out a breath as he got out of her vehicle. "I'm remembering a better time— in my life," he clarified, "not in comparison to tonight. I had a good time," he admitted as they came to his door.

She pretended to be impressed. "Wow, and I didn't even have to pull any teeth to get that out of you this time."

He shook his head. The woman never stopped, he thought. "You're relentless, aren't you?"

She took no offense at his assessment. Actually, she took it as a compliment, though she had a feeling he hadn't intended it that way. "I'm one of seven and the runt of the litter. I have to be."

Runt. Now there was a term he would have never applied to her. "You're not like any runt I've ever seen."

"Thank you—I think," Kari added with a soft laugh.

He didn't even crack a smile. It was far too hard to smile when his gut felt as if it was twisted into a knot. *Breathing* was a challenge. And all because she was standing so close to him, the moonlight in her hair and the scent of her perfume encircling him like a golden lasso.

"Don't thank me for the truth."

He'd lived the past three years in the shadows, doing his best not to be noticed, remaining off the grid and unappreciated. He needed to know that what he thought mattered, she realized. That his whole life didn't just amount to footprints in the sand.

"Someone has to," she told him softly.

Drawing a breath was no longer important to him. But, as he stood there before his door, he knew that kissing her *was* important to him at this very moment in time, even if it wound up being his last, dying act.

So, the next moment, he went with his instincts and did what he'd been longing to do for *hours* now.

He kissed her.

Chapter 14

Hallelujah!

The singular declaration of thanksgiving and joy echoed in Kari's head as she rose up on her toes and wove her arms around Esteban's neck, eagerly surrendering to the sinfully delicious sensations that were shooting throughout her body.

It brought with it a wave of incredible relief.

She'd become convinced that if anything was going to happen between them, *she* would have to be the one who made the first move. Since they'd gotten into her car, Esteban had been so stoically quiet she'd assumed he was silently counting the minutes until she would drop him off at his apartment and leave him be.

But if that had happened, it would have left her grappling with unresolved feelings and an itch that desperately wanted to be scratched.

However, neither choice open to her would have been satisfactory. To make the first move would have been awkward for her. To go home a seething cauldron of unaddressed desires would have been even worse.

Now, mercifully, she didn't have to force herself to pick either.

Because Esteban had just ended her dilemma and sent her hurtling through space, all aglow like a comet.

And then, just as abruptly as Esteban had begun kissing her, he stopped.

All the oxygen had been drained out of her lungs—possibly out of the area surrounding her, as well. Kari stared at the man responsible for her condition, dazed and temporarily unable to string together two words to create even half of a coherent thought.

Blinking, Kari ran the tip of her tongue along incredibly parched lips in an effort to separate them so she *could* say something—once a thought actually came together in her head.

"Well…okay…good…night," she said, stumbling through the simple words.

Esteban had somehow managed to open his apartment door while she was trying to remember if English was indeed her first language. Rather than take the opportunity to just disappear into his apartment or mumble an inaudible response, Esteban took hold of her hand and tugged on it just enough to get her to follow him inside.

Pushing the door closed behind her, the man who had unknowingly made her tingle all day backed her up against that same door. Then, his hands braced against it on either side of her, he completely filled up all the available space around her just before he brought his mouth down on hers again.

Her heart had already started pounding hard again a microsecond before their lips met.

But that didn't hold a candle to the rhythm it hit once Esteban kissed her again. It began beating so hard that, in comparison, a rocket would have seemed to be going in slow motion.

Esteban stopped for a second time, even as all systems were gleefully proclaiming to be a "go" inside her.

"At this rate—" she struggled hard to catch her breath and not gasp out her words "—my accelerator is going to stall out or break altogether."

"I just want to be sure it's not the alcohol," Esteban told her, his eyes holding her in place.

She wasn't sure what he was asking her. Did he think his judgment had gotten clouded because he'd had a few drinks? "For me or for you?" she asked.

"You." Had he been the one to imbibe too much, he had enough control over himself to stop what he was doing and insist she go home. But he was worried that *her* resistance had been compromised.

Kari's eyes held his as she struggled with the very real desire to just rip off all his clothes and end any need for further discussion.

Her voice was low and husky with raw desire as she said, "I stopped drinking four hours ago."

His eyes scrutinized her. "Then you're sure?" he pressed, giving her every chance to shut him down.

"Let me think." Kari pretended to give his question serious consideration. That lasted exactly one second. "Yeah, I'm sure," she told him with feeling.

"Good," he pronounced.

That was all he wanted to hear—to be sure that he wasn't just taking advantage of her or the moment, that he wasn't pressuring her into something she wasn't fully prepared for. Had she opted to walk away, he wasn't certain what he would have done to cope with her rejection. He knew only that he would have had to deal with it somehow.

But he was very grateful he wasn't going to have to find out how.

Even so, Kari had managed to awaken a hunger in him that hadn't reared its head in so long that he couldn't remember it—the last time he'd actually been with a woman. But Esteban forced himself to rein in his eagerness. He made himself go slowly so that they could both savor the moment, rather than making love as if they were swirling about on the outer funnel of a twister, forced to blast through it before they were both unceremoniously thrown to the ground. That way wouldn't have been memorable, only fast.

He wanted it to be memorable.

And perforce Esteban had no intentions of taking her right here, by the front door, even though his body was more than ready to do just that.

Instead, his mouth still sealed to hers, his desire for her so red-hot it was almost sizzling, he began to move backward, forcing her to match him step for step, going in small, measured steps that would eventually lead them into his bedroom.

And while the unorthodox two-step was going on, he was undressing her, coaxing the silvery straps off her slender shoulders, tugging the shimmery material down her upper torso.

When the top portion of her dress had dipped to her waist, she felt Esteban's mouth curving against hers. He was smiling, she realized incredulously.

"What?" she breathed, wanting to know what could have made him respond this way. Was he smiling? Or was he actually laughing at her?

She didn't want to believe the latter.

"Just as I thought," she heard him murmur as his palms cupped her breasts. "You're not wearing a bra."

Her eyes met his and he saw a positive wickedness come into the blue orbits. Her laugh was low and sultry and instantly wove itself underneath his skin, tantalizing him.

"That's not all I'm not wearing," she whispered just before her lips returned to his.

She'd fallen behind in the war on clothes and worked now to make up for it, pulling his jacket off his wide shoulders, then going on to attack his jeans, unbuckling, unbuttoning and pushing the denim down his taut hips and off his thighs.

She heard him catch his breath, *felt* his anticipation as it throbbed through his loins.

Her pulse accelerated as she felt her own anticipation heightening.

They'd made their way into the middle of the living room, a trail of his clothing marking the path. He had yet to explore the meaning behind her statement about more missing articles of clothing.

Steeling himself, holding tightly on to his last shred of control, Esteban pulled her dress farther down her torso, easing the fabric along her hips to discover that the thong he expected to see on her was nowhere to be found.

"Commando," he murmured, referring to her lack of underwear.

"Seemed somehow appropriate," she said, her breath hot along his skin, pushing him to the brink and then over.

Sweeping her up into his arms, his mouth sealed to hers again, he carried Kari to his bedroom.

Gently depositing her on his rumpled gray comforter, he slid his body down next to hers, never fully breaking their contact or the rhythm they had achieved.

His very blood heating within him, Esteban kissed her over and over again, growing more and more excited with each and every pass.

He caressed her body, his touch gentle, his fingers spread out as if he were committing all parts of her to memory as quickly as he could. He could almost feel the flames of desire licking his body as he pressed it closer to hers.

Wanting to absorb her very essence, to almost devour her, he kissed her face, her eyes, her throat, her shoulders. Sampling, teasing, arousing, he worked his way down along her breasts, her waist, her navel.

His pulse racing, Esteban paused for a moment to regain control over himself. Inadvertently, he saw how her stomach muscles quivered in response to the warmth of his breath as well as to the touch of his tongue as he lightly stroked her with it.

He saw desire flare in her eyes as she arched into him and reached for him, wanting to hold him closer to her, wanting to all but crawl inside the sensations he had stirred within her.

They were within the center of the tornado and he held off the final moments for as long as he could.

Longer, he had the impression, than Kari apparently wanted to withstand.

Grabbing him by the shoulders, she choked out a

single word, "Now," and it sounded for all the world like an order.

He would have laughed if he hadn't wanted her so much that it filled every single tiny available space within him.

So, rather than try to muster enough breath to offer a flippant retort—or any retort at all—he drew himself up slowly along the length of her body, allowing her to realize just how completely he wanted her.

His body fully positioned over hers, Esteban saw that her eyes were shut.

"Look at me," he commanded, saying the words so softly, she didn't seem to hear him at first. Her eyes remained closed, as if she was immersed in a fantasy world all her own.

"Look at me," he repeated, his voice a little firmer, the words a little louder.

This time, he saw her eyes flutter open with a start, as if she expected something to bring about a crashing end to what they were experiencing together.

"Why?" she asked, her voice low and husky—and surprisingly teasing. "So I can identify you in the lineup later?"

Was she ever *not* flippant? he found himself wondering. The look in her eyes didn't belong to the woman who had just uttered that quip, and yet, when Kari spoke, it was as if there was a wall between them. A small one, granted, but it was there nonetheless.

Separating them.

You do the same thing with your silence, a voice inside his head pointed out.

The hell with it, he thought. Now was not the time to wage internal debates or search for the meaning behind gestures or deeds. Now was the time to relish what was right here before him.

Right here before *them.*

"My eyes are open," she prompted. "Why does it matter to you if they are or not?"

He didn't answer her.

Not verbally.

Instead, gathering her closer in his arms, Esteban drove himself into her, wanting, just for a moment, to lose his sense of self and create something entirely different. Wanting to create, however temporarily, a union.

He took pleasure in the ache that was being released, in the feeling of fulfillment springing up all around him. He didn't want to let those sensations go.

He'd made love with women before, so many that he'd lost count. He'd made love to more beautiful women, even more accommodating women.

But he'd never wanted to make love with a woman as much as he did right at this moment. With *this* woman.

The ride they went on was brief in the ultimate scheme of things, but while it existed, it raised them up to the very top of the world, allowing them to look down on all that was spread out before them.

The resulting euphoria burst out and encompassed everything, seeping into all corners of life. It seemed to stay suspended in midair for a long, endless moment.

And then, just as with all other things, it began to recede. To shrink into itself and retreat until all traces of it ever having existed faded quietly away.

He lay beside her, unable to examine his thoughts or to assess the myriad of feelings that were bumping up against one another, leaving him in a dazed stupor. The condition was not without its appeal.

Rather than pull away or withdraw into himself, Esteban realized that he had slipped his arm around her and had actually pulled her to him, acting like a longtime lover instead of a stranger who had paused to dally but should have already begun to move along on his way to the rest of his life.

He didn't want to move along to the rest of his life. He liked it where he was and wanted to remain a little longer. That wasn't too much to ask, was it?

"I think I could grow to like Cavanaugh weddings," he confessed as he stared up at the ceiling.

He felt her quiver slightly beside him. He thought at first that she was cold, but then he realized that she was trying to contain her laughter. Unsuccessful, she finally allowed the sound to burst out as she gave full vent to it, laughing so hard that her very sides shook and tears came to her eyes.

Raising up on her elbow, Kari looked down at the

man who had completely rocked her world. Doing her best to catch her breath, she struggled to form words.

It took another minute before she could finally tell him, "I'll be sure to tell Uncle Andrew that you said that."

Her eyes were bright with laughter, and the tips of her hair teased his chest in sync with her laughter. It aroused him all over again—something he hadn't believed was possible, at least not so soon. It had certainly never happened to him before. Not like this, not this strong.

Reaching up for her face, he threaded his fingers through her hair, cupped the back of her head and said, "Later. Tell him later," just before he brought her face back down to his level and kissed her again.

She more than willingly agreed, silently saying yes in her head because her lips were otherwise occupied at the moment.

Chapter 15

The sound crept into her consciousness slowly, growing identifiable by degrees.

Initially, all Kari was aware of was the passion that was burning yet another fiery path through her, just as deep, just as intense, as the first one. All she wanted, all she could focus on, was attaining that incredible, ultimate high that they had generated together earlier. The pursuit of that caused her to block out everything else in her surroundings.

Which was why the sound of the cell phones, each with its own unique ring, didn't register with her at first. Outside noises, a passing car racing by the com-

plex, all these were distractions she was actively keeping at arm's length.

All she wanted was to keep making glorious, teeth-
jarring love with Esteban.

But the ringing continued, insistent, demanding,
scratching its way through the barriers she'd set up. By
the fourth time around, Kari recognized it for what it
was. Reality, knocking the foundations out from underneath paradise.

With a sigh, she lifted her head, drawing her lips
away from his, and looked into Esteban's blue eyes.
She saw regret there, mingling with resignation. It
mirrored her own.

"It's not my imagination, is it?" she asked with a
sigh. "You hear it, too."

Shifting her body to the side so that it no longer
covered his, Esteban raised himself up on his elbow
and glanced at the floor from his vantage point. He
didn't see his cell phone.

"Sounds like our phones are ringing," he confirmed, although, for the life of him, he didn't know
where either device was currently located.

Just loud enough to be heard, both ringtones
sounded too faint to be in the same room with them.

Having no choice, Esteban got up. Kari shifted and
turned so that she was facing the bedroom doorway
and watched the man who had just made incredible
love to her leave the room. She knew he was going to
look for the cell phones. Despite the possible gravity

of the situation—she could only think of one reason why both phones were ringing at the same time—she couldn't help allowing her mind to wander for a moment, lost in utter admiration.

Any way you looked at it, the man had an absolutely gorgeous body.

"Mine's in my purse," she called out, remaining where she was. "By the front door."

Her purse had been the first thing she'd dropped the second she was inside his apartment. Any remaining barriers had been completely incinerated at that moment.

Within a few seconds, Esteban was walking back into the room, just as magnificently uninhibited as when he had gone out.

He held her purse with its ringing phone out to her even as he was answering his own.

"Fernandez," he said, then listened to the voice on the other end of the persistent call.

Sitting up on the bed, Kari had taken her own phone out and announced to her caller, "Cavelli-Cavanaugh." The moment she finished saying her full name, the voice on the other end of her phone began talking. "Okay…be right there," she promised.

She ended her call at the same time that Esteban finished his. She could tell by his expression that the calls had been identical, apprising them that a fourth body had been found.

So much for hopes that the serial killer was finished.

She sighed, shaking her head. "Talk about bad timing."

"You talking about us or the call?" Esteban asked her, wondering if she was having regrets about hooking up with him. He was willing to take the blame if she was, even though he hadn't pressed it. But he was the scoundrel and she was the princess in this setting, so the blame naturally fell to him.

Kari thought of being facetious and saying, "Both," but then decided, for once in her life, to play it straight. To stop constructing protective walls around the most vulnerable part of her heart. So she told him the truth. That she was sorry they'd been interrupted. "I was talking about just the call."

He looked at her for a second, and she thought he was going to say something. But if he was, he apparently changed his mind. Instead of talking, he caught her by her shoulders again and kissed her.

The contact was fast and hard, and maybe she was wrong, but she could have sworn there was a promise there. A promise that tonight wasn't isolated. That there would be another time for them.

Just not now.

Collecting herself, she squared her shoulders and declared, "Okay, let's get to it. We've got a body waiting for us."

He rolled his eyes at her as he threw on a pair of

jeans and put on another pullover. "I don't think it's going anyplace."

Question is, she thought as she slipped her dress back on, *are we?*

"Wow, you really didn't have to dress up for me," the M.E. said, whistling when he looked up and saw Kari heading toward him. He was in the latest victim's living room, examining a body that was still faintly warm.

"Don't worry, I didn't," she said. "My father got married today," she told him, then amended, "I mean yesterday."

"Right, sorry I missed that," the medical examiner said. "But someone had to stay on duty and hold down the fort." His gaze swept over her slowly, scrutinizing her outfit. "Looks like it must have been some party," he surmised.

Something stirred within Esteban, a protective instinct that rose to the surface in light of the look of discomfort on Kari's face.

"Never mind that," he snapped. "What can you tell us about the body?"

The M.E. looked surprised to hear Kari's partner say anything at all. "He's dead."

"Besides the obvious," Kari pressed impatiently.

"That Hal Rockwell was a damn fine judge," a deep, solemn voice said behind her.

Kari turned around to see who was talking. The

voice had sounded familiar, but she'd dismissed her first impression because she knew she had to be mistaken.

Except that she wasn't.

"Blake?" she asked uncertainly, looking at the tall, dark-haired man walking toward her. Blake Kincannon was a judge, one of the two who had married into the Cavanaugh family. Blake was married to Greer, another one of the Chief of D's nieces. As far as major crimes went, this one had just taken a quantum leap.

The next moment, she saw Greer coming to join her husband. Dressed in jeans and a light blue windbreaker, the detective filled them in on what she'd learned from talking to the victim's live-in housekeeper, Amanda Foster. Returning from visiting her sister, it was Amanda who had discovered the judge's body and called the police.

Greer and Blake had attended the wedding earlier, although the couple had left before she and Esteban had. Kari nodded at them now, and if the woman noticed that she was still wearing her dress from the reception, Greer tactfully gave no indication of it.

"A few dozen more Cavanaughs and we can recreate Uncle Sean's wedding," Greer commented dryly.

"No disrespect intended, but what are you doing here?" Kari asked the couple. "Does the Chief think we need reinforcements?" If so, she could understand why Greer was here, but why send the judge, as well?

"After the housekeeper found him, she was so

panic-stricken that she called Blake before she even called the police," Greer told her.

"Hal and I are old friends," Blake explained, picking up the narrative. There was a heaviness in his voice that was impossible to miss. "When I first sat on the bench, Hal was my mentor. He went out of his way to take me under his wing, teach me everything he knew. This shouldn't have happened to him," he said angrily, looking back at the body.

"Could this have been the work of someone he sent to prison?" Kari asked.

"There's always that chance," Blake admitted.

Suddenly, he locked eyes with Greer and they exchanged knowing looks. Although the couple was blissfully happy now, their romance had gotten off to a perilous start. Kari recalled how it was a death threat that had brought Greer into Blake's life in the first place. Fortunately, all that ugly business was behind them now.

Blake cleared his throat and then continued. "In our profession, we all live with the possibility of vengeance, but I can tell you that Hal Rockwell was the most honest, the most decent judge I ever had the pleasure to work with. Once they'd served their time and got out, he helped a lot of the folks he'd sentenced to prison find work and rebuild their lives, as long as they demonstrated a willingness to turn over a new leaf."

A selfless person. Just like the first two victims, Kari thought, although not the third. None of this was

making any sense. Could they have all been living secret lives, part of some secret society that ultimately
led to their deaths? Instead of answers, she was grappling with more and more questions.

"Would you mind if we came by tomorrow to ask
you a few more things about the judge? You know,
pick your brain after you've had some time to get a
good night's sleep?" she suggested to Greer and her
husband.

"I don't think I'll be getting much sleep tonight,"
Blake speculated.

Greer slipped her hand into his, silently offering
Blake her support. "Let's go home, Blake," she urged.
"We won't be much help and we'll only get in the
way right now." Very gently, she guided the judge
away from the crime scene. But before she left, she
made eye contact with Esteban. "Get this bastard,"
she mouthed.

Saying nothing, Esteban acknowledged her request
with a nod.

It was enough.

Despite the fact that she was still wearing the silver
cocktail dress, Kari decided to go straight to the squad
room with Esteban rather than making a pit-stop at
home to change into something more functional. The
hope that this latest victim would somehow cause the
dominoes to finally fall into place outweighed her

need to throw on something that was a bit more comfortable than the slinky evening dress.

Kari pinned the latest victim's photograph next to
the others and started a fourth column listing what
they knew so far.

"Maybe once we get a chance to talk to Blake, we'll
find that common denominator we're looking for," she
said to Esteban.

"What if there isn't one?" he countered. "What if
our serial killer is just some certifiable crazy who
slashes people's throats whenever the mood strikes or
he perceives some slight—real or imaginary?"

She refused to even consider that possibility right
now.

"No, there's got to be something, some trigger,
something about *these* people rather than all the other
individuals he comes across in his day-to-day life that
turns him into a homicidal maniac. At the very least,
there has to be some common place where their paths
cross." Kari stared at the board. There wasn't *nearly*
enough information under each victim for them to
work with. "It's going to drive me crazy until I figure
it out," she said, more to herself than to him.

Kari sank down in front of her computer, pulling
up the files she'd compiled on the first three victims,
and tried to see if there was any sort of overlap, any
common links between any of them and the judge.

Completely immersed in her search, she wasn't
aware that Esteban had stepped away from his desk

until she swung back around to answer the phone on her desk.

Where had he gotten to? she wondered as she said into the phone receiver, "Cavelli-Cavanaugh."

"Put your traveling shoes on, Hyphen," the lieutenant's deep voice rumbled into her ear. "There's been another one."

"You're kidding," she cried in disbelief. Nothing for almost a week and a half, and now two in one day? What *was* it that drove this killer?

"I never kid before dawn, Hyphen," he told her sardonically, then rattled off the address he'd just received. "Oh, and before you start complaining about being overworked, I'm filling out the paperwork to get you and Fernandez a task force to help you with this case. Just because you've got two names doesn't mean I expect you to do twice as much work. You got any problem working with Donnelly and Choi?" he asked, naming two detectives attached to another section of the department.

"Donnelly and Choi will be fine," she told him, then asked with a glimmer of humor, "Haven't you heard? I'm easygoing."

"Yeah, right." He laughed shortly. It wasn't a pleasant sound. "And the sun rises in the west. Get yourself over to the crime scene, Hyphen."

The line went dead. The lieutenant wasn't much for hellos or goodbyes.

Kari sighed, hanging up just as she saw Esteban

walking back into the squad room. He was carrying a covered coffee container in each hand.

"Thought you might need this," he explained, setting one cup down in front of her on her desk.

Kari rose to her feet and picked up the container. "Don't take the lid off," she told him as he was about to sit down and get comfortable. "We just got a call that there's been another murder."

He stared at her for a moment as if she'd lapsed into another language. "You're kidding."

"Same thing I said," she told him, grabbing her purse. "Unfortunately, the lieutenant was serious."

Esteban put his hand on her shoulder, stopping her before she could stride out of the squad room. "You look beat. Want me to drive?" he asked.

"Coffee, chauffeuring. If I didn't know any better, I'd say you were being nice to me. I'm not dying, am I?"

"Not that I know of," he deadpanned.

She took a breath, forcing herself to deal seriously with what she took to be the situation. "Look, I just want you to know I don't expect any special treatment just because—well, just because," she concluded. They were alone, but the squad room was no place to talk about this in any kind of detail.

"Duly noted," he told her. "But for the record, you do look beat. The offer still stands," he said. "Want me to drive?"

She liked being in control, had fought for it for half

her life. But sometimes it was nice to have someone else take over and carry the load. Maybe this was one of those times.

"I won't say no," she said.

"First time for everything," Esteban commented. His expression gave no indication that he was pleased. He put his hand out for the keys.

After a beat, Kari surrendered them.

"You were right, you know," Esteban stated quietly several miles into their trip to investigate the latest crime scene.

"Of course I was," she said with feeling. When he gave no indication that he was going to clarify what he meant, she was forced to ask, "About what this time?"

He carefully picked his way through what he considered a minefield. Each word brought with it a memory, memories he didn't feel equipped to deal with. "About knowing me from high school. I did go to the same school you did, and I was the football quarterback."

Kari reminded herself that she wasn't supposed to know any of his backstory between the end of high school and the moment he'd walked into the squad room. It wasn't easy. But keeping that in mind, she asked the first logical question that would have occurred to her under those circumstances.

"Why did you lie about it?"

He looked straight ahead at the road, his expression stony. "Because I buried all that a long time ago."

She told herself to leave it alone, but would he have expected her to? She ventured forward cautiously, testing the waters as she went.

"Mind if I ask why?"

"Because everyone I cared about was alive back then, and if I think about that, then I have to think about their deaths and the pain hits me all over again," he said fiercely, struggling with his emotions. "I can't go through that. It's better just to leave everything buried."

She knew he wasn't asking her for advice, but she gave it anyway—because she could see he was in pain and she wanted to help.

"Those people you loved, they wouldn't want to see you like this," she said gently, trying to appeal to his sense of logic. "They'd want to see you try to be happy."

Happy was not a sensation he was well acquainted with, not anymore. Happy had been another state of mind, locked away in his youth. The very best he could hope for, he thought, was not to be too miserable.

And nothing Kari with her hyphenated names could say was going to change that.

"Leave it alone, Kari," he ordered gruffly.

About to continue with her argument, she stopped when it suddenly occurred to her. "You realize that was the first time you called me by my first name?"

He snorted. Leave it to her to pick up on just that. "Won't happen again," he promised shortly.

Kari sighed. "You are a hard nut to crack, Esteban," she told him.

He liked it better when she called him by his last name. It made it less personal somehow. "I wouldn't try if I were you," he warned.

There was nothing to be gained for her. He wasn't about to shed his frog skin and become a prince for her if she said just the right words.

She smiled at him. It was that wicked smile that got under his skin. Now that he'd made love with her, he was even less immune to it than before.

"But you're not me," she told him. "Maybe once this investigation is over," Kari suggested, "we should give walking a mile in each other's shoes a try. Who knows…it might go a long way toward building a strong partnership."

Not to mention other things, she added silently.

He glanced down at the silver-heeled sandals she was wearing. "As long as the shoes I have to walk in aren't those damn high heels you have on."

She pretended to scrutinize them, then looked over toward his feet. "Oh, I don't know, from what I saw, you have pretty decent legs. You might even look cute in them."

"Let it go, Hyphen," he gritted out.

Too late, she thought. But rather than continue exchanging witty banter, all she did in response was smile at him.

He found that even more unsettling than her banter.

Chapter 16

"He was an assistant district attorney?" Kari asked the man who had called the police to report discovering the body of the latest murder victim.

Still pale and shaking, investment broker George Springsteen squeezed a yes out of a throat that sounded like it was about to close up on him any second now. He looked apprehensively at the long black bag containing his longtime friend as two of the medical examiner's assistants wheeled it out of the victim's den on a gurney.

"We had a…a date to play tennis this morning," the stricken broker said, struggling to maintain control over his voice. "Philip is—was—never late. He was obsessive about that." The breath he blew out sounded more like a shudder. "When he didn't show up at the court and didn't call me, I knew something had to be wrong."

"Wrong?" Esteban questioned the ashen-faced man. "What do you mean by 'wrong'?"

Springsteen shrugged helplessly, his expression saying that it all seemed so insignificant now. "A flat tire, his ex-girlfriend showing up at the house, making a scene, that kind of thing."

Kari picked up on the angle immediately. There was always a chance that this murder was done by someone taking advantage of the current spree and had nothing to do with the serial killer they were pursuing.

"She has a temper?" Kari asked the broker.

Taking in another deep breath, Springsteen nodded numbly. "She was always on him about something. That's why he broke it off with her." He stared at the wooden floor where he had stumbled across his friend's body, his pallor growing even whiter. "But I didn't think she would do something like—like this."

Now that she gave it a little thought, neither did she, Kari decided. For one very important reason. But all bases had to be covered, so she asked, "Can you describe her?"

Springsteen looked as if his thoughts were scattered in a hundred different directions. It took him a moment to pull himself together enough to form some sort of answer.

"I don't know...five-three, a hundred pounds maybe, give or take. I'm not good at this kind of thing," he protested.

"You're doing fine," Kari assured him in a kind, soothing voice. "Given your description, you wouldn't really say she was a big-boned, strong woman, right?"

"Ria? Hell, no." The laugh that escaped his lips was devoid of any humor. "If she was any thinner, she'd look like a walking beanpole. She's fanatical about not looking fat."

She exchanged looks with Esteban and could tell by the look in her partner's eyes that they were on the same page. The ex-girlfriend couldn't have slashed the A.D.A.'s throat so cleanly. That would have taken a certain amount of strength, strength a lightweight couldn't have managed.

That wasn't to say, however, that, inspired by the recent series of murders, she hadn't *hired* someone to slash her ex-boyfriend's throat, Kari thought.

"Would you happen to have an address and phone number for this Ria?" Esteban asked the distraught broker.

He nodded numbly. "I haven't deleted it from my phone yet." Taking his phone out, he pulled up the woman's phone number. Below it was her address. Springsteen offered his cell to Kari as he sighed deeply. "I guess I should take George's number off my directory, too."

"I don't think he'll be taking any more calls," she told the dead man's friend gently.

"I've moved on," Ria Long snapped indignantly when Kari asked if she remembered the last time she'd been in contact with her former boyfriend.

The painfully slender young woman was standing in the doorway of her modest town house, the gossamer robe she had on barely covering all her assets as a breeze teased the material.

"What's this all about? Philip send you over to plead his case?" she demanded haughtily, tossing her long brown hair over her shoulder. "Too bad. He had his chance."

"So you *don't* remember when you saw him last?" Esteban pressed.

The dark-haired woman smiled like a predator spotting a new prey as her eyes swept appreciatively over Esteban.

"A week ago. I saw him a week ago. He brought my stuff over and dumped it on the doorstep. The spineless jerk thought I wasn't home, but I saw him slinking off. Why?" she wanted to know, her eyes narrowing as she honed in on Kari. "Did he say I took something?" She instantly became defensive. "That watch was mine—it belonged to my father. I gave it to Philip as a token of my love, but I don't love him anymore so I took it back. If he—"

Kari cut the other woman off before she could get

carried away, telling her curtly, "This isn't about a watch."

"Then what's with all these questions?" Ria demanded, fisting one hand on her almost nonexistent hip. "What's going on?"

"Ms. Long, where were you between the hours of twelve and three?" Kari asked, citing the approximate time of death the medical examiner had provided.

The woman looked from Kari to Esteban and then back again. It was obvious that her indignation hadn't allowed her to connect the dots yet. "In bed. With my new boyfriend."

"This new boyfriend have a name?" Esteban queried.

Ria gave up flirting and rolled her eyes. "Of course he has a name. Donald Barry. Now, why are you giving me the third degree?" she wanted to know. And then it finally hit her. Her eyes darted suspiciously back and forth between the two detectives. "Did something happen to Philip? Is that why you want to know where I was? Did he tell you I *did* something to him?"

Kari wrote down the other man's name. They were going to have to speak to him in order to verify the alibi they'd just been given.

"I'm afraid he's not saying anything anymore." Kari faced the A.D.A.'s ex-girlfriend, hating the words she was about to say even though she'd taken an instant dislike to the woman she was talking to. The words were never easy to utter, because, in most cases, they confirmed the worst fears of the person on the receiving end of them. "I'm sorry to have to be the one to tell you this, Ms. Long, but Philip Watson was murdered sometime between midnight and three a.m. this morning."

Ria's dark eyes widened in shock and disbelief. "No. You're lying. This is some sick joke of Phil's to get me to stay away. He's not dead," the woman shouted at them, tears of fear springing to her eyes even in the heat of her anger. "He *can't* be dead. He can't be!" Dissolving into despair, she crumbled to the floor, sobbing uncontrollably. "He can't be," she repeated hoarsely, saying the words to herself rather than to them.

"Either she is one hell of an actress or that was on the level," Kari said nearly an hour later as she and Esteban drove back to the precinct. Getting her second wind, she was behind the wheel again and, at the moment, annoyed with herself for feeling sorry for the woman they had just left in the arms of her current boyfriend. The latter, it turned out, had been in her bedroom the entire time they had conducted their interview with Ria on her front doorstep.

"Yeah, I was just thinking the same thing," Esteban told her. "For what it's worth, I think she's innocent. This was definitely our slasher striking again."

Kari nodded, slanting him a surprised glance as

she came to a stop at a red light. "Wow, we agree on two points. This is almost scary."

Whatever he was going to say in response was put on hold because his cell phone was ringing. Shifting slightly, he took it out of his pocket and looked at the screen.

Still waiting for the light to change to green, Kari saw that he was staring at the small screen. It looked to her as if he was debating letting the call go to voice mail.

"You want to take that?" she asked, guessing the problem. "I promise not to listen."

He startled her by laughing at her offer. "Like you could help listening."

"I'll hum," she told him, then gave him a short demonstration as the light turned green.

Esteban held up his hand as he pressed the green bar on the lower part of the screen, allowing the call to come through.

"Please," he requested, "don't bother." And then he was completely focused on his caller. "Hello, everything all right?"

He sounded concerned, Kari thought. Questions popped up in her head, all sorts of questions regarding not just the identity of the caller but who this person was to Esteban. Was there a lasting bond between the caller and him? Was this an old girlfriend, someone he'd met in his undercover days, or was this someone from his other past…the one he had before he went into deep cover?

Oh, God, was that *jealousy* that was pricking at her? she wondered in dismay. Seriously? In the middle of the biggest case she'd ever handled, after just one torrid night, she was actually being possessive? What the hell was going on here? she silently demanded. This wasn't like her.

Get a grip, Kari, she ordered herself as she struggled *not* to listen to one half of the conversation going on right beside her.

It wasn't easy, despite the fact that Esteban had lowered his voice and the vehicle she was driving did not offer a smooth, quiet ride. It was as if her ears had automatically gone on high alert, even in the face of her initial good intentions.

Esteban was still talking to whoever had called him when they pulled up in the precinct's parking lot. Bringing the vehicle to a stop in the parking space set aside for the car, Kari finally heard her partner saying goodbye.

"Everything okay?" she asked mildly, doing her best to sound disinterested but polite. Given her inherent curiosity, it took a lot of effort to pretend to distance herself this way.

Esteban didn't answer her immediately, as if he was first weighing each word before putting them to use.

"Yeah, he just likes to check up on me every now

and then. His good behavior earns him extra phone time," he told her.

She realized that a sense of relief had washed over her at the use of the pronoun "he." It wasn't another woman.

"Good behavior?" Kari echoed as a second question occurred to her. Good behavior made it sound like Esteban was either talking to a young child who had to earn his privileges or someone calling from prison.

The latter possibility reminded her of something that the Chief had revealed when he'd filled her in on Esteban's family history.

Something she wasn't supposed to know about yet.

Her mind scrambling, she worded her question as best she could. "You know someone on a short leash?" she asked him quietly.

He surprised her with his straightforward answer. "I know someone in prison. My stepfather."

Ordinarily, Esteban wasn't given to sharing. Now that he had, he waited to see if the woman was going to be judgmental of the man who made up the only family he had left. But the look on her face didn't show any sign of censure.

"Why is he in prison?" Kari asked, giving her partner an opportunity to open this door he'd just cracked a little further.

Giving him the opportunity to trust her.

He hadn't talked about it in years. Hated talking about it, even though he understood the deed, because talking about it brought all the memories back so vividly. Reminding him that there were things he was powerless to fix.

Finally, he said, "He killed his son's supplier. My half brother, Julio, died of a heroin overdose," he told her bluntly. "Miguel was grief-stricken. He went to the police, tried to get the dealer arrested for killing Julio. But there was no proof, so they couldn't do anything. That was when Miguel decided he would.

"He bought a gun, found out where the guy was dealing, walked up to him and blew his brains out." He said the words, as devoid of emotion as his step-father had been when he had killed the dealer. "Then he went back down to the police station and turned himself in," he told Kari grimly.

Listening, Kari watched his face as he spoke. It was hard and unyielding, lacking any sentiment. But she saw his jaw tightening as he relived what he was telling her.

"He didn't even *try* to get away. He told the police that he did it for Julio—for all the Julios who would have gone on to die if this dealer had gone on selling heroin." Esteban let out a long breath before continuing. It was the only sign that talking about this was taking a toll on him.

"The jury convicted him, but they asked the judge for clemency." It was at that point she saw a trace of bitterness mark his features. "The judge was hard-assed, though. Said Miguel's reasons didn't matter. He did the crime, he had to do the time. Made me want to go after him myself," he confessed. "Instead, I volunteered for an undercover detail being put together. I wanted to try to even the odds up a little myself. For Julio and for Miguel."

The story had moved her emotionally, making her feel for Esteban and helping her understand him a little better. Her heart truly ached for the man, who had endured so much pain and suffering, and it was clear to her now how his past had shaped him into the person he was today. But his harrowing account had done more than just fill her with empathy. It had made her think of something.

"That's it," she cried, her eyes shimmering with intensity. "That's got to be the common thread."

Esteban looked at her. He had no idea what she was referring to. "Going undercover?" he questioned.

"No, a trial. A trial's the common thread. *Think* about it," she stressed. "Who are our victims? A retired judge, an A.D.A. and, according to his friend, one of the victims was bent out of shape because he had to serve on a jury sometime in the past."

They already knew all that. "So?" Esteban questioned.

"So maybe they were all involved in the *same* trial. I bet if we dig deep enough, we'll find that victims one and two either served on the same jury, or were witnesses in the trial, or had *something* to do with it.

That's got to be it—a trial that they all had in common," she concluded excitedly.

It was more than possible, Esteban thought. *If* they could find a common trial. "You think someone they each had a hand in sending to prison is exacting revenge now that he's out?"

That would be the most logical guess, but she wasn't putting all her eggs in that one basket just yet— and she wasn't about to go to the lieutenant with her theory until they'd researched the possibility first.

"Maybe," she allowed, doing her best to keep her voice level and contained. "But first let's see if we can connect these people to a single trial," she told him. And then, unable to be cool and restrained about it any longer, she allowed her excitement to burst out again. "We're right," she cried. "I can feel it in my bones. We're right."

"*You're* right," Esteban pointed out. He'd never been one to take or share credit unless it actually belonged to him. "This was your idea."

Kari was in a very generous, magnanimous mood. She had a *really* good feeling about this. "Which I wouldn't have had if you hadn't just shared your story with me," she told him. Pausing, she sobered a little. "Thank you for trusting me enough to let me in," she said softly. She pressed her lips together, and then smiled at him. Her eyes were bright. "We really are a team, aren't we?"

He smiled at her, brushing back the hair from her

face, feeling the same stirrings taking hold that he'd experienced the night before. He wanted her. God help him, he wanted to take her here and now. In broad daylight. Out in the police parking lot.

"I'd like to think so," he said huskily.

Just like that, Kari could feel longings spring up within her, demanding attention, seeking fulfillment. Her throat grew dry. "If this winds up panning out, I'm baking your stepfather a cake with a file in it."

She heard Esteban laugh, really laugh, at her spontaneous comment. It was a very rich, seductive sound. "You're a Cavanaugh—you're not supposed to talk that way."

"I'm a Hyphen," Kari reminded him, falling back on the nickname she was growing accustomed to. "That gives me leeway," she told him. She saw that he was looking around, first to the right, then to the left. "What are you doing?"

"Checking the parking lot for witnesses," he told her.

"You're afraid someone'll overhear and turn me in?" she asked, amused. That wasn't like him, she thought. But she liked the idea that he was being protective—even if she could take care of herself.

"No, I just don't want anyone to see."

She didn't understand. What was he talking about? "See what?" she asked.

Satisfied that the parking lot was empty, he turned back to her. Despite the way he felt, Esteban didn't want to risk compromising her reputation in any manner. She was the one who mattered in this.

The only one who mattered.

"See me do this," he answered.

Then, before she could ask just what "this" was, Esteban surprised her by leaning in and kissing her.

With very little effort, the kiss could have blossomed and led to a great deal more, but for now it had to hold him, to satisfy him with the knowledge that there would be more later.

"You, Fernandez," she rasped as he drew back, leaving a space of less than six inches between them, "are really just full of surprises."

He smiled then and she could feel the effects go straight into her bones. "Good. Nothing worse than being predictable and dull."

"No chance of that," she assured him, doing her best not to sound as breathless as she was.

As it was, it took her a moment before she felt that her knees were strong enough to hold her up. Only then did she get out of the car.

Even so, it was only by concentrating on the breakthrough she felt they had made on the case that she was able to put one foot in front of the other and *walk* up the back steps to the precinct's rear entrance rather than float up.

She had, she told herself, a good feeling about this. *All* of this.

Chapter 17

"You're back," Brenda Cavanaugh said when she looked up from her work the following morning and saw Kari and her partner walking into the tech lab. "And you brought a friend," she noted as they headed straight for her. "Esteban, right?" she recalled with a smile. "Not sure if you recognize me, since you were introduced to a lot of Cavanaughs on Saturday, but we met at the wedding."

Esteban nodded, politely returning her smile. "I remember. How are you doing?"

Brenda shifted her eyes toward Kari. "I don't know. That depends on what your partner here asks me to do."

Kari became the soul of innocence. "Can't I just be visiting?"

Brenda choked back a laugh, then said, "No."

"Okay, you're right," Kari allowed, then added with emphasis, "this time. But I'll drop by just to say hi next time," she promised.

"I'll look forward to it," Brenda quipped, then went on more seriously, "Meanwhile…?"

Kari had learned a few tricks since her academy days and knew how to phrase things so they were presented in the best possible light—and were almost impossible to turn down. "Brenda, how would you like to save the Aurora Police Department hundreds, maybe thousands of man-hours?"

Because her skills put her in such demand, Brenda had evidently heard it all when it came to detectives trying to wheedle their work requests to the top of the pile. But the receptive look she shot Kari implied that Brenda was willing to hear her out.

"So far, so good," the computer tech responded. Then, humor curving her mouth, she bluntly asked, "Exactly where is this going?"

Kari took out her folder containing a copy of the photographs of all the victims with their names and either former or present occupations written beneath their images. Since there'd been no one available in the tech lab yesterday when she'd come up with her theory, she and Esteban had made the rounds questioning the judge's and the A.D.A.'s neighbors, as well as several of their separate friends, starting with Greer and Blake.

Just as she had suspected, absolutely no one had seen anything or anyone who aroused their suspicions. The workday had ended in frustration.

The night, however, had been a whole other matter. There had been no frustration there, just a late dinner and a great deal of lovemaking. No matter where she and Esteban wound up going from here, she was always going to cherish what amounted to an utterly exquisite weekend.

But it was a new day now, the beginning of a new week, and she wanted to bring down this serial killer so badly she could almost taste it. And although Esteban said little on the subject, she could sense that he felt exactly the same way.

"I—we," she corrected, glancing toward her partner, "need you to cross-reference something for us. We need to find out what case A.D.A. Philip Watson pleaded before Judge Hal Rockwell."

Brenda couldn't help but laugh. "You make it sound so simple, but that's not one case. My guess is that we're looking at a whole bunch of cases," she said, pulling the folder closer. Her eyes swept over the other photographs and she raised a quizzical eyebrow.

Which was when Esteban told her, "There's more."

Brenda sighed. "Of course there is. Go on," she said, waiting to be filled in.

"The case in question involved this man serving

on the jury." She moved the third victim's photograph closer to Brenda. "And it's possible that these two people were also on the jury." He moved the photographs of the first two victims and had them join the third victim's. "But we're really not sure yet just how these two fit in with the rest—other than being this serial killer's victims."

"Well, I'll say one thing for you," Brenda declared. "Your request is colorful, not to mention challenging." She looked over the information that Kari had brought her in the folder. "Okay, this is going to take me a while."

"Not nearly as long as it would take us if we had to wade through all the boxed archives in the courthouse basement," Kari assured her. "Thanks, Brenda, we owe you."

"That's what they all say. Someday, I intend to collect. Big-time," she told them, pretending to put them on notice.

"It'll be worth it," Kari assured the older woman as she and Esteban left the tech lab.

Kari had exactly fifteen minutes to feel good about her hunch before her cell phone began ringing. She knew without looking that it couldn't be Brenda getting back to them so soon.

And she was right.

Taking her phone out, she had just enough time to

answer before the voice on the other end of the call said something that had her jaw dropping.

"So soon?" she cried, disheartened.

She'd really hoped that, with Brenda's help, they could get to the killer and stop him before he honed in on his next victim. But the serial killer had beaten them to the punch.

Again.

She closed her eyes, fighting back a wave of frustration.

"Yes, sir, yes. Fine." She opened her eyes again, slanting Esteban a quick glance. "He's right here with me. Yes, right away." With the call abruptly terminated, she slipped her phone into her pocket. "We're not going up to the squad room," she informed him.

"Another one?" It was a rhetorical question. He'd guessed the content of the call by the look on her face.

"Another one," she echoed. "The bastard's upping his game much too fast. Of course," she added, trying desperately to find a silver lining to this, "the faster he kills, the more likely he is to make a mistake." And when he did, she was going to *get* him. Big-time.

"That's not much of a comfort to his victims," Esteban said brusquely.

Kari sighed, her frustration mounting at a prodigious rate. "I know."

The moment they found out the latest victim's occupation, Kari immediately got back in contact with

Brenda. This *had* to mean she was right, she thought excitedly.

As soon as she heard the line on the other end being picked up, she immediately started talking, struggling to sound relatively coherent. "Those court cases you're cross-referencing…" she began.

"And hello to you, too, Kari," Brenda said with a laugh.

"Hello," Kari returned the greeting belatedly. "Add Attorney James Bell to that list I gave you earlier."

There was silence on the other end for a moment and then Brenda asked quietly, "Is he…"

It didn't take a genius to know what the rest of the computer tech's question was. "The latest victim, yes," she responded, then said more eagerly, "There *can't* be too many cases involving all three of those men. Once you've found those, you can use the reluctant juror to complete the weeding-out process."

"I know my job, Kari," Brenda reminded her good-naturedly.

The last thing she wanted to do was insult her new cousin-in-law and the Chief's daughter-in-law to boot. She was just so eager to have this all finally come together, she was tripping over her own tongue—and stumbling across other people's feelings.

"Sorry, Brenda," she apologized. "I didn't mean to insinuate that you didn't."

"Apology accepted," she said, evidently taking it all in stride. Kari knew that the older woman was all too familiar with the emotional roller coaster that detectives rode while working their cases. "Oh," Brenda added offhandedly, "and tell Esteban that I wish him lots of luck."

Kari didn't understand. "Why?" she wanted to know.

"I think he'll understand" was all Brenda said before she ended the call.

"She find something?" Esteban asked the moment Kari put her phone away.

She realized that she was furrowing her brow as she pondered the other woman's odd words, so she forced a neutral expression to her face. "Not yet—but she said to tell you that she wished you luck."

Rather than ask her what Brenda meant by that, the way she assumed that he would, she saw Esteban laugh, compounding the mystery for her.

"Then you *do* know what she's talking about?" she asked him.

He wasn't positive, but he had a pretty good idea. "My guess would be that she thinks you come on a little too intense and dealing with that on an ongoing basis a minimum of five days a week might be…a little *challenging* for me."

"I want to catch a serial killer before he winds up wiping out half the city," Kari protested. "What's wrong with that?"

"Not a thing, Hyphen, not a thing," he told her with an easy smile she found hopelessly sexy.

Concentrating on her job was getting harder and harder for her, Kari thought. Especially when torrid memories of last night and the night before kept unexpectedly ambushing her mind.

She did her best to block those thoughts, but she was fighting a losing battle.

Shortly after she and Esteban finished eating the takeout they'd picked up for lunch, Kari's cell phone rang.

For once, she didn't immediately take out her phone. "Oh, God, if that's someone calling with more bad news, I don't think I can stand it," she moaned.

"Well, it's not the lieutenant calling," Esteban told her. He nodded toward the man's office. "He's not on the phone."

"Okay, maybe that's a good sign." Mentally crossing her fingers, Kari pulled out her phone. "Cavelli-Cavanaugh."

"I think you need to come down here."

She recognized the voice immediately and mouthed "Brenda" to Esteban. For once containing her all-consuming curiosity, Kari didn't instantly bombard the other woman with questions. Instead she replied, "We'll be right there."

"It *is* another body?" Esteban wanted to know the moment she ended the call.

"No," she answered. "From the way Brenda sounded, I think we've just had a breakthrough," she said as she rose to her feet and all but *flew* out of the squad room.

Caught off guard, Esteban found he had to lengthen his stride just to catch up. "You know, for a little thing," he told her once he was abreast again, "you can really move."

Just for a second, she allowed herself a quick mental detour. Flashing a wicked grin, she said, "I thought you already knew that."

His laugh made her gut tighten with hopeful anticipation about the night ahead. "I'm learning, Kari, I'm learning."

She loved hearing him say her name, but she knew better than to admit that to him. If she didn't say or do anything to scare Esteban off, maybe whatever it was that was going on between them would last awhile longer.

At least she could hope.

"We're here," Kari announced, walking quickly into the tech lab. The eager note in her voice was impossible to miss. "Are you going to make our day?"

"Quite possibly," Brenda replied. She doled out the information in stages to allow the two detectives to digest it properly. "First off, I found your connection. Judge Rockwell, A.D.A. Watson and that defense attorney, Mel Samet, were involved in a number of cases—"

Kari could feel her stomach begin to sink. "How many?"

"Twenty," Brenda told her.

Observing the exchange, Esteban scrutinized the look on Brenda's face. There were traces of triumph there. That could mean only one thing. "How many cases with that guy on the jury?" he wanted to know.

Brenda laughed. "Cut to the chase, right? To answer your question, one." As Kari started to inundate her with questions, Brenda held up her hand, asking for patience. "But that's not the most significant part."

"Go on," Esteban urged. One glance at his expression told Kari that he was still expecting to hear the worst. She needed to rub off on him a little more, she thought. He'd be a happier man for it.

Brenda went over the details as quickly as possible, hitting only the highlights. "The trial involved a rape case. The teenager accused of raping this girl was tried as an adult, convicted and sent to prison. His father tried to get the verdict appealed. The kid kept protesting that he was innocent."

"That's what they all say," Esteban commented darkly.

"True," Brenda agreed. "But it turned out he really was. The real rapist was this repeat offender who could have been the kid's twin. They caught him on another charge, the guy confessed and the original verdict was overturned." She paused, looking distraught by what she was about to reveal. "The only problem was it was too late. The same day that the verdict was being overturned, the kid was killed in prison by another inmate." Brenda glanced at them before adding the last piece of important information. "His throat was slashed."

So much for thinking an ex-con with a grudge was killing the people responsible for sending him away. "But if the poor kid's dead, then who's killing all these people?" Kari wanted to know.

Before Brenda could answer, Esteban thought of his stepfather and said, "His father."

Clearly impressed, Brenda turned to Kari. "I'd say this guy's a keeper."

"I'm leaning that way myself," Kari told her. She meant to make it sound like a joke, but she wasn't quite successful.

Suppressing a knowing smile, Brenda got back to business. "The kid's father took it hard and swore revenge on the justice system," she informed them. "I guess this body count was what he meant."

It certainly looked that way to her, Kari thought. "You have an address for this man?" she asked the other woman.

"Would I let you down?" Brenda asked. Taking a page the printer had just spat out for her, she handed it to Kari. The page contained a copy of Ray Gibson's DMV license. On it were his picture and his address.

"You're the best, Brenda," Kari declared as she

folded the paper and slipped it into her back pocket. "C'mon, Esteban, we've got a killer to detain."

They lost no time leaving the lab.

Ray Gibson's apartment, once they gained access to it with the aid of a reluctant superintendent, was empty. Judging from the date of the newspaper left open on Gibson's beat-up kitchen table, the man had left three weeks ago—exactly the time when the killings had begun.

Framed photographs of Gibson's deceased son occupied almost every flat surface available, dating back to when he was a baby.

The entire apartment had been turned into a veritable shrine to the teen. There was a photograph of father and son—the only one as far as they could determine—on the cheap coffee table.

Esteban paused before it, picking it up and looking more closely at father and son.

"You find something?" Kari asked, coming over to join him.

He'd been studying the older man's face, trying to remember where he'd seen it before—and then it came to him. "I've seen this guy before. He was the stenographer at my stepfather's trial."

She didn't bother asking if he was sure. She knew Esteban well enough now to know he didn't say *anything* that he had the least doubt about. Seeming reckless, he was actually as stable as a rock.

"I guess we can stop wondering how he got his hands on the names and addresses of those three jurors." Her eyes widened as a thought hit her squarely between the eyes. "Oh, God."

Esteban had just had the same thought. "He's got the rest of the addresses."

She nodded numbly. "We're going to need those extra detectives that Lieutenant Morrow promised me," she said. They had possibly a great deal of legwork before them and speed was of the utmost importance. "Immediately," she added.

Her first call was to Brenda, followed by a call to the lieutenant.

Armed with the names and addresses of the remaining jurors who were still alive and in the area— one juror had died of natural causes, another had drowned in a boating mishap and three had moved to other states—Kari divided up the remaining four jurors, giving three to the other detectives that had been temporarily assigned to her department. She took the fourth one, a Kyle Masters, for Esteban and herself.

With luck, they could get to all four before the killer did.

While Esteban drove them to the fourth man's house, Kari called the cell phone number Brenda had provided for the juror.

All three tries went to voice mail.

"I've got a bad feeling about this," Kari told her

partner as she gave up trying to reach the man by phone. "Drive faster."

Esteban pressed down harder on the accelerator.

Chapter 18

There was no answer when they knocked on the door of Kyle Masters's single-story house.

"Maybe he's at work," Kari said. But even as she said the words, she had a sinking feeling in the pit of her stomach that she was wrong.

Esteban had moved over to the window that was adjacent to the door and peered in. The see-through curtains at the window afforded him a view into the living room.

"Not today." He grimaced. "There's a body lying on the floor in the living room...and my guess is that it's his."

They were too late, she thought, frustrated. "We need to kick down the door."

"Much as I'd like to watch you try to do that," Esteban told her, "I've got a better idea."

"Okay, I'm listening," she prodded.

But rather than answer her, Esteban moved her out of the way, then took something out of the wallet in his back pocket. Inserting the match-thin metal into the lock, he began to work at the lock.

Approximately ninety seconds later, the door was unlocked.

Kari suppressed the impulse to whistle her admiration. "Very nicely done," she told him as she prepared to go in.

He grinned at her. "I learn from the best," he told her with a wink that, despite the gravity of the moment, made her heart flutter.

Later, she promised herself. *I'll think about this later.*

Right now, they had a serial killer to catch.

He saw Kari take a deep breath as she trained her gun dead center at the door. She was psyching herself up. So was he.

"Ready?" he asked, his voice dropping to hardly a whisper. He slowly twisted the doorknob, easing the metal tongue from its groove.

"Ready," she mouthed, accompanying the word with a nod of her head. Adrenaline was surging through her at incredible speed.

The next moment, in one quick motion, Esteban pushed the front door all the way open. Every fiber of her being was on the alert as Kari entered the seemingly empty house.

But the second she crossed the threshold, she felt her left arm suddenly being grabbed from the side. And then a hunting knife, still covered in the latest victim's blood, was being pressed against her throat, the tip nicking her skin as she was dragged backward and to the side.

"Don't come any closer!" a frenzied voice behind her threatened Esteban. "I'll slash her throat just like I slashed his. It's your call."

"Put the knife down, Mr. Gibson," Esteban said in a reserved, calm voice that belied the turmoil that was churning inside him. "You don't want to do this. We're police detectives. You don't want to hurt her."

"No, but I will," the distraught man cried, his voice rising and on the verge of cracking. "Unless you put your gun down, I will."

"Don't listen to him, Esteban," Kari ordered. "Take the shot. He's going to kill us both if you put your gun down. Take the shot!"

Esteban never took his eyes off the man. "Is she right?" he asked in the same monotone voice he'd used before.

His mind raced, frantically searching for an alternative, a way out for Kari. But the knife the man held against Kari's throat was almost drawing blood. Gibson could kill her in an instant.

The horror of that thought almost paralyzed him,

all but making him physically ill. He couldn't lose her, he *couldn't*.

"Will you kill us both if I put my gun down?" Esteban pressed, his tone flat, devoid of emotion.

There was hysteria in the other man's voice. "One thing's for sure. I'll kill her if you don't."

Oh, God, Kari thought, Esteban was wavering, she could see it in his eyes. They were both lost if he bought into this.

"Don't," Kari cried. "Don't do it. He's killed at least seven people—"

"They deserved it!" the man interjected, screaming the words.

"What's to stop him from killing two more?" she pointed out, completing her thought and praying Esteban listened to her.

"Can't risk it," Esteban said to her. Then, very slowly, he lowered his weapon to the floor.

Okay, it was now or never, Kari told herself. The man with the stranglehold on her waist had nothing to lose by killing them. All she could think of was that she couldn't let that happen.

With a wild, guttural cry, she suddenly used both hands and grabbed the arm that was holding the knife to her throat. Adrenaline pounded through her veins even faster as the pain of a sharp prick registered.

Focused only on one thing, she sank her teeth into Gibson's wrist. The blood-curdling shriek almost made her deaf. She thought he'd screamed because she'd bitten him, but then she felt Gibson's hold around her waist loosen and realized that his body was sinking down behind her.

His knees hit the floor, and as she jumped aside, she saw the rest of him go down, face-first, on the rug.

That was when she finally swung around to look at Esteban, who was also on the floor. It took her a split second to realize that with Gibson momentarily distracted, Esteban had dived to retrieve his weapon, and from his awkward position on the floor had shot the deranged man.

Scrambling up to his feet now, Esteban was beside her in less than a heartbeat, his hands on her shoulders. The deadly calm expression was gone from his face, replaced by one of mingled fear and concern.

"Are you all right?" he demanded hoarsely.

She pressed her lips together and nodded. Something was hurting, but she'd probably gotten banged around. "Never better," she cracked.

"He cut you," Esteban gasped, staring at the blood he saw oozing along her throat.

She touched the wound gingerly and winced. "Oh, yeah. I guess he did. It's just a flesh wound," she assured him. Glancing at the man who was lying facedown on the floor, she saw the pool of blood that was forming a red outline around his head. "Nice shot," she commented. Her eyes shifted back to Esteban's face. She'd never seen him look so pale. "I take it that wasn't just a lucky shot."

"Yeah, it was," he told her.

He'd been shaking so badly inside, he'd been afraid that he would hit her instead, even though he'd had sniper training, thanks to the department.

And then unable to cope with the thoughts that were attempting to crowd into his head, thoughts that all had to do with the devastating consequences they'd have faced if he hadn't managed to get off that single shot, Esteban just pulled her into his arms and held her close.

She resisted to an extent. "I'll get blood all over you," she protested.

"Shut up," he told her, emotion throbbing in his throat. Emotion that, until now, he'd managed to keep locked away. "Like I care."

She clung to him, all resistance gone. His presence gave her tremendous solace, and his warm, comforting embrace provided her with the strength she needed at a time like this.

"We need to call this in," she reminded him after a few moments had gone by.

"We will," he assured her, his arms tightening. "I just need a second."

"Yeah," she admitted quietly. "Me, too."

The CSI unit, along with Lieutenant Morrow and the other detectives he'd temporarily reassigned to the task force, all converged on the scene, almost en masse. It took a minimum of detail to fill the lieutenant in.

"I guess he just went off the deep end when his son was killed in prison just after the judge reversed the guilty ruling," Kari said. "He wanted to make everyone involved in sending his son to prison suffer the same fate his son had," she said solemnly. "He wrote on his son's social media page that he was on 'a mission from God,'" she told Morrow. That was something one of the other detectives had told her just before the lieutenant had arrived.

"Too bad nobody picked up on that and alerted us sooner. Some of these poor bastards would have still been alive if they had," Morrow commented. "Good work, you two," he congratulated them. "One last order for the day and then you're both free to go home and get some rest." He looked at Esteban intently. "Take her to the hospital to have that looked at." He nodded at the bandage on the side of her neck.

"The paramedic already looked at it," Kari protested. "He put some disinfectant on it that hurt like hell and then bandaged it."

The lieutenant looked unimpressed. "I'm not going to be the one to explain to the Chief of D's why he's short one niece." His eyes shifted toward Esteban. "Take her. Now!" he underscored.

"You heard the man," Esteban said, taking her by the arm and firmly guiding her to where they'd left their car at the curb what seemed like a hundred years ago.

"I've got a better way for you to 'take' me," she

said, echoing the lieutenant's order and putting her own meaning to it.

"Later," he promised her. "First we get that taken care of."

"What if I say no?" she challenged.

He was prepared for that. "Then I'll have to throw you over my shoulder and carry you there."

A smile entered her eyes. "Can I opt for that?" she asked.

"Shut up and get in the car," Esteban ordered gruffly.

"Make me," she countered, curious to see just what he would do.

Rather than pick her up and *put* her in the car the way she expected him to, he framed her face with his hands and kissed her. Kissed her with all the unbridled emotions that were running rampant through him, all the fear he had dealt with in those split seconds when he'd seen the deranged serial killer put his knife to her throat.

Kissed her as if there was no tomorrow, only this moment, only now.

She went from solid to liquid in under forty seconds, her insides vibrating like a well-struck tuning fork.

When Esteban finally drew back, she all but collapsed into the car. Unable to stand, she definitely needed somewhere to sit.

"You fight dirty," she accused.

"Only way I know how to fight," he informed her.

His answer made her smile. "This is going to be a very interesting partnership."

He spared her a long look before pulling away from the curb. "I was just thinking the same thing."

Which meant, she thought in sudden realization, that he wasn't going anywhere. He was going to stay in her life.

Esteban reached inside the door to his apartment and turned on the light, then stood back to allow her to enter first.

Coming inside, Kari smiled. "It looks a lot better in the light. Dusty, but better." She turned toward him. "I'm just curious, why did you bring me here?" she asked. "Why not to my place?"

"Because mine's closer and I'm a man of my word."

"Oh?"

"Yes. I said I'd take you to bed, remember?"

Her mouth curved. "It was the only thing that kept me from running out of the E.R."

Esteban smiled at her bravado as he drew her into his arms. "That and the fact that they took your clothes."

Kari laughed. "If you think that stopped me from running out, then you don't really know me at all."

"Maybe," he allowed for the sake of argument. "But I plan to."

The next moment, he covered her lips with his own.

The kiss was long and deep and did a great deal to blot out everything else that had happened in the past twelve hours.

She sighed as she felt Estaban draw back for a moment. "More please," Kari murmured.

"As you wish."

But instead of kissing her again, Kari felt herself being lifted up off the floor and into his arms.

"What are you doing?" she asked, surprised.

"Guess."

The wicked look in his eyes made guessing completely unnecessary. Kari knew exactly what he was going to do. And she couldn't wait for it to happen.

It was a good long, steamy hour and a half before any more words were exchanged between them.

Lying next to Esteban in his rumpled bed—a bed that had already been rumpled before they ever started making love—Kari turned her body into his and said, "I think you might just have stumbled across a new way of treating wounds."

He did his best to look serious, but failed. The desire to grin was just too overpowering. "Good to know—for the next time."

The next time.

She clung to that for a moment, savoring what it could—and should—mean before making herself ask, "Does that mean you've decided to stay on as my partner?"

"I'm thinking about it," he replied softly—and

then his grin gave him away. Shifting so that his body curved into hers, Esteban grew a little more serious. "I don't know what it is about you, but for all your annoying little traits, you still made me think that maybe there's some hope left for this world."

Pleased beyond words at this change in him, for the sake of the game they were playing, Kari pretended to take offense. "What annoying little traits?"

"We'll review them some other time. Right now, I'm more interested in going over your redeeming ones—the ones that redeemed me," he added quietly.

That touched her heart more than she could possibly ever express. "Esteban? You think that the next time you go to see Miguel, I can come along?"

He realized that he'd like that, that he wanted his stepfather to meet this woman. But he still needed to know why she'd want to come with him.

"Why?"

"Because I'd like to meet the man who had a hand in making you the person you are today."

He felt his heart swell and cautioned himself to take it one step at a time. These emotions were new and he needed to work up his trust.

His bid for nonchalance failed, though, as he said, "Sure, why not?"

Still trying to be cool, she couldn't help thinking fondly. Esteban's answer made her smile. "You know I see great things for this partnership."

Just before he kissed her again, he said, "I was just thinking the same thing."

Kari would have grinned if she were able, but seeing as how her lips were definitely otherwise occupied, she didn't.

There was time enough for grinning later.

Epilogue

It was another Cavanaugh wedding.

This time it was Kari's sister, Kendra, marrying Matthew Callaghan, the detective whose mother had married Kari and Kendra's father last month.

This, Esteban had said to Kari when she told him about the upcoming nuptials, put a whole new emphasis on the term *family ties*.

But another Cavanaugh wedding meant another pulling-out-all-the-stops celebration. And this time Esteban found himself really looking forward to attending rather than feeling it was just something he was forced to put up with.

"So, Detective Fernandez, are you enjoying yourself?" Kari asked after extricating Esteban from a small group of men comprised of two of her brothers as well as a couple of her cousins, one of whom was also Brenda's husband, Dax.

Esteban looked at her appreciatively. The floor-length light blue gown she had on adhered to every curve and made him think of one of the goddesses straight out of Greek mythology. He couldn't recall ever thinking of a bridesmaid's dress as being sexy. But that was the word for this one.

And for her.

"I am now," he confided.

"Good," she said, taking him by the hand and drawing him onto the dance floor that had once more made its appearance in Andrew Cavanaugh's spacious backyard. "Then dance with me."

"Are bridesmaids allowed to dance with civilians?" Esteban murmured, taking her into his arms and swaying to the music. "Aren't you supposed to be dancing with one of the guys standing up for your brother?" he asked. "The guy they paired you up with?"

He'd been surprised just how much it actually bothered him, seeing her walking down the flower-strewn aisle with another man at her side. It had set him thinking.

"Groomsmen," she supplied the term for him. "They're called groomsmen."

"Yeah, those guys." He deliberately pretended to play dumb, slowly leading up to his point. "Aren't you just supposed to be dancing with one of them?"

She laughed, wondering if he was actually serious.

But then, she gathered that there hadn't exactly been many weddings in his world before he'd become her partner. Only funerals.

She winked at him. "I won't tell if you won't."

"I don't want you breaking any rules on my account," he told her with a perfectly unreadable expression.

"That wouldn't be because you don't want to dance now, would it?" she asked him. Because, reluctant or not, the man was really a wonderful dancer. He had natural rhythm—unlike a couple of her brothers.

"Not want to dance?" he repeated incredulously. "What red-blooded American male wouldn't jump at the chance to have an excuse for putting his hands on you in public?"

Kari laughed and shook her head. "Ever the gentleman."

"That's me," he agreed, loving the way they moved together.

"You didn't really answer me before—are you enjoying yourself?" she asked him again. "At my father's wedding, you told me after it was over that you'd had a good time." She'd caught him looking strangely introspective a couple of times during the ceremony. "Is this one not measuring up?"

"Oh, it's fine," he assured her. "It just made me think."

Was this going to be bad? Was he going to tell her that he'd decided he needed to be alone, to move on, maybe go somewhere else...away from painful reminders of his past? "About what?"

"About what I'd want if this was my wedding."

Stunned, she could only stare at him. Finally finding her tongue again, she heard herself ask, "And what would you want if this was your wedding?"

He looked into her eyes and said quietly, "Something more intimate."

She tried to read between the lines. *Were* there lines to read between? She didn't really know. "You mean less people," she guessed.

He nodded. "I think an intimate group of, say, ninety to a hundred would be my limit. Give or take," he added with a hint of a smile beginning to curve the corners of his mouth.

Exactly what was he trying to say? "That doesn't sound very intimate. That sounds like—"

"Your family?" he asked, the smile blossoming completely.

"Well, yes." He wasn't saying what she thought he was saying—was he? Men like Esteban ran from things like that, didn't they? "About this wedding..." She wasn't sure just how to proceed.

He twirled her around the floor, never taking his eyes off her face. "Go on."

She drew her courage to her, hoping she didn't sound like a babbling fool in the process. "Is it something that might be happening anytime, you know, like soon?"

He inclined his head, as if he was thinking. "Well, that all depends."

She could feel her breath backing up in her throat, all the while telling herself not to get too carried away. If she was wrong, the fall back to reality would be excruciatingly painful.

"On what?" she breathed.

"On when you'll say yes."

Her heart was pounding so hard, it made it difficult for her to talk. "*When,* not *if?*"

Esteban looked at her for a long moment. "You're going to make me beg, aren't you?"

Oh, God, no, she didn't want him changing his mind. "Not beg, but it would be nice to hear a few words."

And he knew which few she was referring to. "You want me to tell you I love you."

That made it sound forced, she thought with dismay. "Well, only if you do…" she qualified.

He shook his head. Did that mean he didn't love her? She felt an icy chill slide down her back.

"I thought you were a good detective."

He had officially lost her. "What does that have to do with it?"

Finding her insecurity adorable, Esteban laid it all out for her. "A good detective would have already realized just how much I love her."

Relief took on the proportions of a tidal wave as it washed over her. It took her a moment to catch her breath and then she urged him, "Tell me anyway."

"Kari Cavelli-Cavanaugh, I love you and I want you to add my name to that long parade of last names you already have." Still swaying with her, he paused and laughed. "And I think we should stop dancing." He nodded toward the band. "The music's stopped."

"No it hasn't," Kari contradicted as she continued dancing to the music in her heart. "And yes."

"Yes?" he questioned. He wanted to be perfectly clear what she was saying yes to.

"Yes," she repeated. Laughter filled her throat. "In answer to your first question. Yes, I will marry you. And in case there's any doubt, yes, I love you." Her eyes were shimmering with tears of joy and she grinned up at him.

"What?" he asked, sensing there was something more.

"Uncle Andrew is going to be on cloud nine when we tell him." Three weddings in three months would make the former chief of police a truly happy man.

In case she had any thoughts of running off to find the man now, Esteban held her tightly in his arms.

"'Uncle' Andrew can wait to find out later," he told her, just before lowering his mouth to hers and kissing her in the middle of the now empty dance floor.

Uncle Andrew, Kari thought as she encircled her arms around Esteban's neck, undoubtedly already knew.

* * * * *

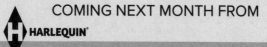

REQUEST YOUR FREE BOOKS!
2 FREE NOVELS PLUS 2 FREE GIFTS!

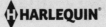

ROMANTIC suspense

Sparked by danger, fueled by passion

Diego unbuckled her harness as Vanessa clutched the helicopter seat's armrests. "What are you doing?"

He pointed across her, out the door. "You have to jump, Vanessa."

Oh, no. Absolutely not.

Clutching the door frame so hard her fingernails ached, she shuffled her feet toward the edge and poked her head out the side to stare at the green water below. Over the roar of the rotor blades, she shouted, "Are you crazy? How high up are we?"

"Fifteen meters. It's as low as I can get with these trees."

Fifteen meters was fifty feet. A five-story building. Her stomach heaved. "There could be barracuda in there, or crocodiles. Leeches, even."

"That's a chance you have to take. There's nowhere else to land. The rain forest is too thick and we're out of fuel. You have to suck it up and jump."

"What about you?"

"I'm going to jump, too, but I have to wait until you're clear of the chopper. And there's a chance my jump won't go off as planned. We're running out of time."

She knew she needed to trust him not to leave her, but it was hard. She'd never been this far out of control of her life and she couldn't stop the questions, couldn't let go of the fear that he'd abandon her to fend for herself. "How do I know you're not going to dump me here and fly away?"

"I thought we went over this. Did you forget my speech already?"

"No." But promises were as fluid as water, she wanted to add. People made promises all the time that they didn't keep.

"You gotta hustle now. We don't have much time left in this bird."

She stood and faced the opening, then twisted to take one last look at Diego. What if he didn't make it? What if this was the last time she saw him? "Diego…"

"Jump into the damn water or I'm going to push you. Right now."

She whipped her head straight. Like everything else that had happened in the past couple hours, with this, she didn't have a choice. She sucked in a breath and flung herself over the edge.

**Don't miss
TEMPTED INTO DANGER
by Melissa Cutler**

Available June 2013 from Harlequin Romantic Suspense wherever books are sold.

ROMANTIC suspense

CONFESSING TO THE COWBOY
by Carla Cassidy

Small town Grady Gulch has been held captive
by a serial killer targeting waitresses.

Mary Mathis may hold the secret to the killings,
but she risks losing it all if she confides in Sheriff
Cameron Evans, a man who has been captivated
by Mary. Will she confess to the hot sheriff
before the killer takes her as his final victim?

Look for *CONFESSING TO THE COWBOY*
by Carla Cassidy next month from
Harlequin® Romantic Suspense®!

Available wherever books and ebooks are sold.

Heart-racing romance, high-stakes suspense!

www.Harlequin.com

HRS278251

The kiss was to scare her away.

Instead, he managed to scare himself—but not before he took the so-called "warning" he was issuing to its full conclusion, devouring her the way a starving man devoured his first meal in countless days. Except that for Esteban, it had been countless months, not days. Countless months that had stumbled their way into years without his complete memory of the empty journey. Pleasures of the flesh hadn't been important to him at the time.

Now, though, something seemed to be waking up within him....

Dear Reader,

Welcome back to the Cavanaugh world, where family is always the most important ingredient and love can break through the thickest walls.

This time we get to meet Sean's daughter, Kari, who not only doesn't have a problem when she discovers that, thanks to her father, she is actually a Cavanaugh, she welcomes the news. Kari has always made the best of every situation, which is why Brian Cavanaugh, the chief of detectives, feels she is the perfect partner for Esteban Fernandez, a former undercover narcotics officer. Esteban's sole purpose in life is to avenge the deaths of his half brother and mother at the hands of the drug cartel. When that is taken away from him, he needs help finding a reason to go on. Kari decides that it is *her* mission to make him come around and see the good he can accomplish working with her as a police detective. She hadn't counted on falling in love with her assignment. But nothing is ever without twists and turns in the Cavanaugh world, and this is no exception.

As always, I thank you for reading and from the bottom of my heart I wish you someone to love who loves you back.

All the best,

Marie Ferrarella